Innocent Assassin

Paul McDonald

Copyright

First Edition July 2022

Second Edition November 2023

Paperback ISBN: 978-0-646-86041-1

Cover Design by Armeia Aguilar

Edited by Regina Smith

Part 1

Present Day

The Interrogation

One

Sakura pushed the kickstand into place with her left heel and leaned the Ducati Monster motorcycle over until the stand took up the weight of the big bike. She had parked in the Coles supermarket underground car park in Bexley, a suburb of Sydney, as it was only a few blocks from her destination. Tonight would be her first kill. Her target, an evil man who preyed on the weak and the innocent.

She could feel her heart pumping in her chest, blood and adrenaline surging, causing a drumming sound in her ears. Sakura smiled; she was excited. Tonight, she would avenge her mother. She had trained the past decade for this night. She pivoted on her left heel and got off the bike.

Sakura was slightly built, only 150 cm tall and weighing just 48kg. However, ten years of martial arts training had sculpted her body, and her muscles were lean and powerful. At first glance, it was easy not to notice her underlying physique, which gave her an advantage as opponents often underestimated her strength and speed. Sakura was a perfect killing machine, able to use her entire body as a weapon.

Her target tonight was Roy who, in contrast to her, was a monster of a man who liked to hurt people, especially women. Roy stood 210 cm tall and weighed 115kg, mostly muscle. He worked out at the local gym five times a week, at least 90 minutes each session. Years of dedication to strengthening his body had provided him with a broad, deep chest, bulging biceps, thick forearms and powerful legs.

2

Sakura locked her helmet to the bike and replaced her bike riding gloves with the thin leather gloves she had carried in her backpack. These gloves had been handmade for her in Japan and were of the finest quality. The leather was supple, allowing her to make precise movements. In addition, the gloves would minimise any bruising to her hands and assist in minimising DNA evidence.

She looked at her watch. It was 6:30pm, twilight when the day transitioned into night. The timing was no coincidence; it's when the eyes are forced to adjust to the diminishing light making it difficult for anyone seeing her to provide an accurate description if questioned by the police. She put her arm through the backpack strap, threw it into position on her back and walked confidently from the car park.

Two

Sakura had arrived from Tokyo two weeks earlier and followed Roy ever since, observing his movements and planning her mission. She had learned that Roy didn't have a regular job; he was a stand-over man, and his income was derived from extortion. Every Monday to Friday from 10:00am to 2:00pm, he would visit small businesses, hair salons, restaurants, cafes, fruit and vegetable stores, massage shops, tattoo parlours, etc. Each day of the week, he would travel to a different area and visit 20 or more businesses, demanding his insurance money.

One day Sakura was able to look through the window of a barber shop and see the barber hand Roy a $100 note. She thought that if each shop had to pay Roy $100, he would generate $10,000 a week, more than half a million dollars a year, tax-free. No wonder he had a beautiful home and a fancy car.

Yesterday, she followed Roy to a Chinese café and waited outside when he entered. Inside was an elderly man. She saw him hand Roy a $50 note. Then she heard the owner telling Roy he could only pay $50 this week. Roy's response was to punch him hard in the nose, then he grabbed the elderly man's right hand, placed it flat against the counter and hit it three times with the wooden mallet used for tenderising chicken. Sakura could hear the elderly man's screams in rhythm with each blow as he begged Roy not to hit him again.

Sakura moved to the nearby bus stop as Roy left the café, yelling at the old man, "I will expect $150 next week or your other hand will get the same treatment." Then Roy walked along the footpath to his next shop and next victim. Sakura got up, turned and walked towards the window of the Chinese cafe. Inside she could see the elderly Chinese man bent over the counter, holding his broken, bleeding hand upright. Tears streamed down his face, and his wife, with her arm around him, supported him from collapsing. She reached for an apron and began to wrap his damaged hand in the apron.

Sakura's face transformed from a frown to a smile.

I will enjoy meeting you, Roy.

Over the past two weeks, she had identified his patterns, and she was ready and confident that her plan would enable her to quickly and efficiently disable the much bigger man.

She would end Roy's life tomorrow.

Three

Sakura walked casually along the path towards Roy's home. During her surveillance of Roy, she had studied the best route from the car park to his house, keeping her in the shadows and away from casual eyes. This preparation had paid off as she had not encountered anyone during the short walk.

Roy lived in a quiet cul-de-sac with leafy footpaths. Each home had a mature Jacaranda tree on the nature strip standing like a sentinel guarding the property. Despite being a cul-de-sac, the road could accommodate parking on both sides while allowing traffic flow. The homes were modern and prestigious compared to the surrounding streets. It was obvious that the people who lived here were financially well off. The gardens were well maintained. Luxury cars were parked in the driveways. She had seen a Mercedes Maybach, a BMW M8, and a Hummer. The street was quiet, with no traffic and no people; it was perfect for her purpose.

Sakura reached down, pretending to tie a loose shoelace. She tilted her head to see behind her without it being obvious. It was clear and she was alone on the street. She stood and walked down Roy's driveway, making her way to the rear entrance of his home.

Shrugging her shoulders from her backpack, she opened it and removed her lock pick kit. Last week she had entered Roy's home to assess the security and study the home layout. Roy had taken precautions for his safety and the rear door was secured by a high-Security BiLock, a solid and challenging lock to pick due to its U-shaped key. Each blade of the key interacts with a bank of six sliders inside the lock, and each slider has a false and an actual gate. Sakura selected a tension bar and a standard 25-hook tool from her lock-pick kit and started on the lock. She opened the door in under 45 seconds, 15 seconds faster than last week.

She removed a small pencil light from her backpack and entered the house, locking the door behind her. She turned on the pencil light, walked through the laundry, and then passed a powder room into the kitchen where she could hear the home security system's slow beep, beep, beep. She walked over to the panel on the wall and keyed in the code to turn it off. During her reconnaissance last week, she had attached a military decryption unit to the security system to determine the deactivation code. As she had expected, Roy had kept the same code.

She turned on the room's lighting which instantly illuminated the area, showcasing the vast open-plan design. She stood in a spacious kitchen, a marble island with six stools separating the preparation and dining areas. The dining area hosted a massive eight-seat wooden dining table, probably built from oak. A six-seat couch separated the dining area from the living and entertainment areas.

One wall boasted a 90-inch OLED TV, the sound delivered from multiple speakers integrated into the surrounding walls around the room. Below the TV was the expensive Klipsch's 8-way sound system amplifier which powered them.

The bedrooms and a study were located on the eastern side of this living space. Sakura had previously selected the study as the room where she would wait for Roy.

Over the past two weeks, all of Sakura's time had been used observing Roy and understanding his routine. During the day he would run his extortion racket. Most afternoons were spent in the gym. Wednesday, he would do his grocery shopping. At night when he returned from the gym, he would pour a bourbon then eat a light meal he had prepared in the morning.

The occupants of the house opposite his home were on vacation which provided Sakura with a perfect observation platform for her to watch him in the mornings and evenings. Roy's life was routine, almost habitual, and she had never seen him with friends. He never had visitors. His lifestyle made Sakura's job simpler.

Sakura walked into the study, opened her backpack and started her preparations. The study provided her with a strategic vantage point. From here, she could see a large proportion of the house. She smiled at the thought that tonight was the night Roy would pay for his evil, lecherous sexual assaults. Tonight was the culmination of a decade of training.

When she had completed her preparations, she returned to the kitchen, activated the security system, turned off the house lights and returned to the study, where she sat cross-legged and waited for Roy to return home.

Images of her mother began to appear in her mind. Her mother had been beautiful, the memory so vivid she could still smell her perfume. Sakura missed her mother; she was taken from her too soon. Her sadness gave her renewed energy for what she was about to do. She took a deep breath, quieted her mind and entered a deep meditative state while waiting.

Fifty minutes later, she was alerted by the rumble of a big V8 engine and the garage door opening. She stood, shook her arms and did a few squats to increase her circulation. She was on full alert now, all her senses heightened. First, she could hear the car enter the garage; then, the engine shut down. After that, the only noise was the whirr from the electric motor closing the garage door and the ticking sound of the engine as it cooled.

Her nerves were tingling. Her heartbeat increased, pumping blood to fuel her muscles, preparing them for optimum performance. She would undergo her first mission in just a few moments, something she had trained for half of her life. Tonight, she would avenge her mother. She was ready, and her remaining thought was that Roy was an evil man and the world would be a better place without him.

Four

Roy was enjoying the rumble of the big V8 under the bonnet of his Shelby 500 GT Mustang as he drove home. He loved this car, a real muscle car that complemented his alpha male image. The 315 Cubic inch engine was supercharged, delivering a tyre-shredding 800 Horsepower. The growl from the modified exhaust could be heard from 300 metres. It was a real head-turner for men and women alike.

Roy was smiling. He felt happy. It had been a good afternoon—first, a solid workout at the gym and then sex with a new woman, which was always fun. Catherine had been flirting with him for weeks at the gym, and tonight was the first opportunity to take her home. It hadn't taken long to convince her they should move into the bedroom. Like most women, when she saw his engorged member, she gasped, looked up at his face and mouthed, Wow! He was much bigger than the average man and this was a familiar response.

At first, she had enjoyed the sex. He had gone slowly and gently but as he got closer to ejaculation, he started to lose control. His thrusting became harder and faster as he slammed his 115kg frame against her most sensitive parts. She had yelled for him to stop, but that wouldn't happen.

Afterwards, he could see he had hurt her, there was blood on the sheets, and she was sobbing from the pain. He said he was sorry and tried to kiss her. She looked at him with disbelief, the corners of her mouth turning downwards into a wolf-like snarl. That probably meant there wouldn't be a repeat night. He dressed and said, "Catherine, I'm sorry; I didn't mean to hurt you, I just lost control."

"Get out now, and maybe I won't report this to the police," she yelled at him. Her face had turned an angry red. He could see she was furious at him, so he just turned and walked out to his car to head home. During the 20-minute drive, he scolded himself for being so stupid. He had liked Catherine, and now he was concerned that she might go to the police. If she did report the incident, he would be in deep trouble. The last time he faced a judge, he was told that he would be doing time in prison if he appeared in his court again for any similar offence.

Over the past three years, five women had filed complaints of sexual assault against Roy. All the women admitted that it started as consensual until he started hurting them. Unfortunately for Roy, his best orgasms were when he hurt the woman. He didn't understand why; it was just how he was made.

He parked the Mustang in the garage, turned off the motor and sighed deeply. He entered his home from the garage, which led into the laundry, and then the kitchen.

Roy thought a bourbon on ice would be just the trick to calm his buzzing body. He had a bourbon most days when he arrived home from the gym; it was his reward for doing the workout. He poured the brown liquid from the Makers Mark 101 proof bourbon bottle over the five ice cubes he had placed into his favourite crystal glass. He loved the sound of the ice cracking as the bourbon's heat caused it to expand. He took a decent swig, swished the liquid around his mouth then swallowed. *Fuck that tasted good.* Then he thought, what a wonderful life I have. He glanced at the clock on the wall; it showed 7:45pm. He was home a bit later due to his fun time with Catherine.

That's when he felt the sting in his neck.
What was that?
A spider bite?
A mosquito?

Almost immediately, he felt nauseous; his legs weakened, his stomach squeezed upon itself, and his vision blurred. He knew then that he was passing out.

Five

Roy slowly regained consciousness. He remembered the sting in his neck and then nothing! He was in his bedroom now, on his bed; he couldn't move. He was restrained. His arms were outstretched, and his legs spread eagle. His head was held back and secured in a manner that also prevented its movement. He realised he was naked. His heart started to pump faster now as he wondered what had happened. Who had carried and restrained him to his bed, and for what purpose? He swallowed hard. He was frightened, terrified perhaps for the first time in his life. That's when the elfin-like girl came into view. She climbed up onto his bed and looked down at him.

"Hello Roy, do you remember me?"

He didn't. *Who was she, and what was she doing here?*

"Roy, I want you to remember back to 2011 when you and four other men broke into my home. You were wearing masks and did terrible things to me and my mum. Things that a ten-year-old girl should never have to endure. You were wearing the big bad wolf mask. That was you, Roy, wasn't it?"

Then she said, "I want you to tell me the names and addresses of the other men who were with you that night. I want you to tell me who murdered my mother and who tried to murder me."

Roy remembered the night; they were high on crystal methamphetamine (Ice) and alcohol and looking for something to do.

Alex had explained the house was in an isolated area and that they could stay for as long as they wanted without being interrupted. They could do whatever they wanted.

They had been there for three hours, indulging themselves with the mother and small girl. Alex had killed the mother and Mark was supposed to have killed the girl. So how could she be here now? Roy's mind was racing from the adrenalin, *fuck you, Mark, I will sort you out for this*, he promised silently.

"I don't know what the fuck you're talking about, you PSYCHO," Roy screamed.

Sakura calmly bent over him, looked him in the eye and said, "Are you sure, Roy? I won't ask again." Roy's fear grew as he looked into her eyes. Her pupils were dark and dilated and the look on her face was cold. It reminded him of the look you would see on a hardened criminal who had done significant prison time and not something seen on a young woman's face.

She slipped away from his vision. He tried to move his head, arms and legs but couldn't. It was then that he felt the pain in his groin. He yelled out, "WHAT ARE YOU DOING?" He could smell burning flesh.

She returned to his narrow field of vision and looked him in the eye again. She was holding up a medical instrument. "Roy, this is a Laser scalpel; it's truly wonderful. It can cut through skin effortlessly and cauterise the veins and capillaries as it cuts, preventing bleeding." Then she held up something for him to see. It was a string of flesh with a hairy lump swinging below it. He realised it was his testicle she was holding above his head.

"Don't worry, Roy, you have another; well, assuming you tell me what I want to know, that is."

His heartbeat raced, his fear now extreme. He could feel beads of perspiration running down the sides of his face. Now he realised the danger he was in. He was being held captive by a madwoman cutting bits of his manhood away.

For the first time, a woman held him in her control, and he was terrified. Roy began telling Sakura everything she wanted to know.

13

Part 2

Ten Years Earlier

The Awakening

Six

Sakura opened her eyes. At first, her vision was just a blur, and then a beige ceiling with a fluorescent light came into focus. She felt weak, and she couldn't feel her arms or legs. It was difficult for her to lift her head and look around. She was in bed, surrounded by medical equipment. There were tubes in her arm and she could smell antiseptic.

There was a knock on the door and a nurse walked towards her. She had a kind face and long dark hair. As the nurse leaned towards Sakura, the watch pinned to her uniform swung slowly outwards.

"Hello, Sakura. I am Natasha Williams. I have been caring for you over the past months. How do you feel?"

Sakura's mind was racing. Did she say months?

Sakura didn't understand why she was in the hospital.

She couldn't remember what had happened. She was finding it hard to access her memories. Her brain felt mushy and confused; it wasn't working correctly.

Where was her mummy?

Why wasn't her mummy waiting for her to wake up?

"Sakura, can you please tell me how you feel," the nurse repeated.

"My body feels weak, my throat's sore, and I'm hungry."

Natasha smiled, "Well, I'll organise something for you to eat." She pressed the call button and shortly after, another nurse entered.

"Michelle, please have the kitchen send a light meal for an 11-year-

15

old."

"Why am I here?" asked Sakura.

"Where is my mummy? I'm not 11 yet."

Natasha dragged the chair towards the bed, sat down, reached out, and brushed a lock of hair from Sakura's forehead. She held Sakura's hand between her hands and smiled. Sakura could feel the warmth of her touch. She could feel it warming her body, beginning at her hand, then moving towards her wrist and arm and it felt so nice. She liked this woman.

Natasha had been anxiously waiting to see if Sakura would wake. Finally this day had come and they would have to tell the little girl what had happened and how her life had changed forever. Sakura would undergo lengthy physiotherapy and psychology sessions to lead an everyday life again. She had been close to death when she arrived at the hospital. She had been stabbed three times in the chest, suffering multiple internal injuries. Her left lung had collapsed and the aorta severed, resulting in considerable blood loss. The knife had punctured her stomach, emptying liquids and food into the peritoneal cavity, resulting in severe septicemia.

She had been raped and sodomised, her tiny body brutalised. The surgeons had tried to repair the damage as best they could, but it was unlikely she would ever be able to have children. They had placed her into a medically induced coma, enabling her body to undergo multiple operations and repair itself.

That was three months ago and Sakura had missed her 11th birthday. Two days ago they had removed the pentobarbital and thiopental from her saline drip to enable her to wake from the coma.

Robin Culp, the sexual assault counsellor, entered the room. Over the past two months, Natasha and Robin had been discussing the best approach for informing Sakura about what had happened that dreadful night. Natasha took a deep breath. Her mouth had gone dry.

Sakura watched Natasha's face change from a smile to a frown.

"Sakura, this is Robin. She is a trained counsellor and will be available to help you overcome your loss. Do you remember what happened to you and your mother?"

Sakura concentrated hard but couldn't remember what had happened to hospitalise her, "I don't remember." Natasha felt somewhat relieved. The best outcome would be for little Sakura to have suppressed the memories from that night. Together, she and Robin had agreed to a partial truth suitable for a young girl to understand and protect her from the horrors of that night.

"Sakura, it's difficult for me to tell you this." Natasha paused, then said, "Five evil men forced their way into your home to steal from you. Your mother fought bravely to defend you, but they were too strong; they killed her. I'm sorry. They also attacked you, inflicting life-threatening injuries upon you. It has taken three months for your body to recover."

Sakura listened, trying to comprehend. She wondered if she was having a terrible nightmare. She looked at Natasha and then at Robin. She could see the sadness in their eyes and felt their pity. She started to cry, the pain of losing her mother unbearable.

Sakura asked, "Have they caught the men?"

"The police forensics found fingerprints and DNA belonging to five males. There was an extensive search, however, no one has been arrested. The authorities contacted your grandfather. He is in Australia and has been visiting you every day. He left just a few hours ago and will return in the morning."

Sakura's father had died in a workplace accident two years ago. He was an orphan and had no relatives. Her mother's family lived in Japan. Both her parents had been taken from her. She was alone in Australia. Sakura thanked Natasha and asked if she could give her some time alone, tears streaming down her cheeks.

Natasha and Robin said goodbye. As Natasha walked from the room, she started to question if the months of treatment to save this little girl had been the right thing to do. Her parents were dead, and her only known relatives were her grandparents, a wealthy family living in Japan. What was to become of little Sakura?

Sakura lay in bed sobbing. She missed her mummy. Whenever she hurt herself, fell and grazed her knee or elbow, her mother would clean the wound and kiss it better. She needed her mother's kisses now more than ever. She had never been this hurt.

Since her father died, her relationship with her mother had grown even closer and more vital. They had been poor yet happy; they had each other. Their furniture and kitchenware were austere, purchased from charity shops. The exception were the two exquisite Japanese porcelain teacups. One had a red dragon wrapped around the circumference, its black eyes bulging, its mouth opened wide, its serpent tongue reaching towards its tail as it tried to bite itself. It was her father's cup. After he died, her mother stored it away, never to be used again. The second cup in the set had a pattern of flowers draped around its sides. Her mother had told her the name of the flower but she had forgotten. The petals' colours were pink. It was a beautiful cup and her mother drank tea from it daily. She would hold it in both hands, as it had no handle, and she would gaze into the cup, a smile forming on her face, her eyes going blank for a moment as she drifted off to another time.

Sakura remembered they were so happy and laughing in the kitchen one spring morning. The sun was streaming through the curtains her mother had handmade and hung over the kitchen sink. The sunlight brightened the thin fabric, enhancing the fruit pattern, a banana, a pineapple, and a pear.

Her mother was washing the breakfast dishes and Sakura was drying. She enjoyed helping her mother and sharing these simple chores. She reached for her mother's teacup which was slippery from the soapy water and too late, she realised her grip was weak, and the cup slipped from her hand and broke into pieces as it hit the hard wooden floor. She screamed, "I'm sorry, mummy, it fell." Her mother dried her hands, put her arm around her, kissed her cheek and said, "It's ok, Sakura, it's just a cup. I'm sure I can fix it."

Together they squatted on the floor and collected the pieces of the broken cup. Her mother placed them on the kitchen table and said, "I'll repair it today." Sakura looked down and saw minuscule pieces of porcelain on the floor, too small to pick up, yet she knew these were integral to the beauty of the cup.

18

That afternoon when she got home from school, she went to the cupboard for a glass and saw the repaired cup. Her mother would have spent hours meticulously gluing the pieces together, yet it was flawed. It didn't fit together correctly. The tiny bits left behind on the floor had mattered. She could see a gap where a piece didn't match its partner, areas where the beautiful pattern had miniature fractures. Her mother never drank from that cup again.

Years later, Sakura discovered from her grandmother that her father had drawn the patterns for the cups and commissioned them to be traditionally hand-crafted by an artisan from a family that had been creating beautiful pieces of pottery and ceramics for six generations. Her father's design was skilfully applied by hand before the cups were fired in the kiln.

He had presented them to Aiko when he asked her to marry him.

As Sakura drifted into her troubled sleep, her last conscious thought was *I am a broken cup, the doctors have put me back together, but the pieces don't quite fit. Bits are missing, and you can see I am damaged.*

19

Seven

In the morning, when Sakura woke, she felt better. She ate breakfast and managed to climb out of bed on trembling legs. She had to support herself by leaning against the wall and eventually completed the two-metre distance from bed to window.

Outside was a cloudless blue sky, starkly bright against the grey of the hospital buildings. The concrete structures framed against the blue sky gave a perception of strength, and this vision made her feel resolute.

She pledged an oath to focus on her recovery and, when healed, seek out those who had killed her mother. She would avenge her mother and get retribution from those involved.

Later, after she had finished her breakfast, two police officers visited to ask her questions about the attack and home invasion. Sakura didn't remember anything of that night and couldn't provide them with any information. She wondered if her memories of that night were missing or hidden away in a deep inaccessible part of her brain.

While eating her lunch she saw a Japanese man studying her. She recognised him from a photo her mother had shown her. It was her grandfather, Hirutu Hotato. His daughter Aiko, her mother, disobeyed him as a young woman. She had eloped with her Italian lover, Enzo Bianchi, who became Sakura's father. Hirutu had become angry with Aiko's decision and severed all contact with her. Hirutu was the oyabun (leader) of the Yakuza Hotato clan. This position made him a very respected and dangerous man in Japan. Sakura's mother had told her a little about her grandfather. Enough to make her feel very scared.

Now he was here.

Hirutu walked to the bed and Sakura held out her arms so he could embrace her. He whispered to her in Japanese, "I am very sorry for your loss, Sakura. My heart is heavy knowing that my pride robbed me of my daughter and granddaughter for over a decade. I will endeavour to make amends for my actions. I will be your guardian for as long as you wish, and together, we will seek justice for your mother."

Sakura said, "Hello, grandfather," in perfect Japanese. Since the age of six, Sakura had been fluent in English, Italian and Japanese. Her mother and father had spoken all three languages in their family home.

***

Sakura commenced each day with physiotherapy in the gym and the afternoon in the pool. She grew stronger. Her weight increased from 25 to 30kg, a 20% gain in four weeks. The nurses were compassionate. They encouraged her throughout the therapy sessions and sneaked treats into her room when she achieved a new milestone. Natasha was her favourite; she had helped fill the gap after losing her mother.

The scars on her body were ugly thick red lines raised above the softer skin surrounding them. She wondered if they would always look like that and hoped they would fade with time. Her tiny chest looked like she had been in a battle. Ten major surgeries had transformed her appearance to resemble a Frankenstein character. She would cry whenever she looked in a mirror at her damaged body. However, this despair only made her more robust and more determined to ensure those who did this to her would have their day of reckoning.

Natasha was amazed at Sakura's recovery and her determination. Despite the pain, she worked intensely to gain strength and mobility. After three months, she was well enough to leave the hospital. On the morning Sakura was to leave, Natasha hugged her in her room. They were both crying, happy that Sakura was leaving the hospital but sad that they would not see each other again.

Sakura's grandfather entered the room, bowed and said, "Nurse Natasha, I am humbled by the care you have provided for my granddaughter. My family is grateful that we have had such a loving woman helping Sakura during this difficult time."

Sakura looked at Natasha and said, "Thank you," kissed her on the cheek and said, "I love you!" Natasha's eyes filled with tears again and she struggled to say, "Take care, Sakura and email me often. I love you like a daughter." She turned to Hirutu and said, "It has been my pleasure. You have a beautiful granddaughter; I have never met a more determined person."

Hirutu had bought a small suitcase for Sakura containing several outfits and shoes. He waited in the corridor while she dressed, and they left the hospital. They stood outside the hospital's entrance and a limousine drove up to meet them. The driver got out, walked around the car, opened the rear door and waited for them to enter. Her grandfather gestured for Sakura to enter first. It was the first time Sakura had been in a limousine and she was amazed at the grandeur of its interior space. Her grandfather sat opposite her, his back facing their travelling direction. There was a magnificent bouquet on the seat next to him.

Sakura asked, "Who are these flowers for?" His face saddened, and he said, "They are for your mother; I am taking you to see her so you can say goodbye." Sakura turned and looked out the window. Tears started to roll down her cheeks.

They arrived at Rookwood cemetery. She recognised it because her father's grave was there. The limousine drove slowly through the graveyard towards the Japanese burial sites. The car stopped and they exited, Sakura's grandfather carrying the flowers. He walked towards a resplendent grave with Sakura following at his side, holding his hand. The headstone was magnificent, 2 metres tall and 6 metres wide, constructed from solid marble. It was glistening white in the sunlight. The engraving was spectacular, a Japanese calligraphy style and the epitaph was cut precisely into the stone. Each letter highlighted in gold paint—the gold lettering contrasting against the white of the marble.

Two names were carved in exquisite detail.

Enzo Bianchi and Aiko Bianchi
Death cannot keep them apart
Forever in our hearts

At the base of the headstone lay two burial plots encased in stone. The grave on the left was constructed from dark granite with a white stripe running through it. The grave on the right was built from beautiful pink granite. Two smaller plaques lay upon the foot of the graves. The one on the left was the gravestone Sakura's mother had placed on her father's grave. The one at the base of her mother's grave was similar in style with the words, 'I will avenge you' written upon it.

Below these words was the Japanese symbol for Sakura's name.

Sakura looked up at her grandfather. He looked despondent and said, "When we were notified of your mother's death, we flew to Australia the next day. I went to the hospital to ensure you had the best surgeons and care while recovering. Your grandmother arranged the funeral arrangements. At first, we wanted to take Aiko back to Japan for burial in our family crypt. However, we decided that she had chosen Australia as her new home. I arranged for your father's casket to be relocated next to your mother's. They will lie here together for eternity."

"I was a stubborn and foolish man. I should have supported your mother's wish to marry your father. I can never make amends for the years I have lost with my beautiful Aiko. The years I could have got to know my son-in-law and granddaughter. Enzo and Aiko are gone forever. I will make amends for my stupidity and selfishness by loving and caring for you, Sakura." Then he handed her the flowers. Sakura walked to the graves, gently laid down the flowers and said, "Sleep peacefully, mummy and daddy," then, with tears flowing, she turned to her grandfather, took his hand and they walked back to the waiting car together.

Eight

Sakura watched through the window as the cabin tilted upwards. The wheels lost contact with the runway and the ground fell away. The vibrations from the power generated by the four enormous Rolls Royce engines were pulsating through her body. It was the first time she had flown on a plane, and this was an A380, a giant aircraft.

Hirutu had purchased two first-class seats so the journey was very comfortable. Sakura enjoyed watching the available movies and was excited about her spacious seat. Too soon, they were on descent and landing in Tokyo. She was in a very different world.

A car was waiting for them and two Japanese men met them and carried their bags to the big sedan. They drove for ninety minutes and eventually stopped at a mansion on Tokyo's outskirts in the Matsudo suburb. Hirutu introduced her to Mirako, his wife and Sakura's grandmother. Mirako hugged Sakura and said, "Welcome to Tokyo, Sakura." She sighed, then said, "I cried for weeks when I heard what had happened to you and my beautiful Aiko. Your grandfather will ensure you can avenge your mother and our family."

Sakura spent the next few days resting in the house. Her room was enormous. She didn't know that people lived in homes this huge. She spent her days walking through the gardens which were comprised of ponds, stone gardens, and hanging gardens. It was a fairyland.

On the fourth day, Hirutu met her at breakfast and said, "Sakura, it is time for us to talk. You have undergone an extremely traumatic experience and repairing your body and mind will require extensive physical and spiritual training. I have arranged for you to travel to Hokkaido's mountains to a great Sohei Temple. Here you will learn the secrets of the martial arts. I have agreed with Master Shi Yan Ming that he will personally train you. I hope you will enjoy this opportunity."

Sakura was thinking, *should I say thank you? Do I get a chance to discuss this?* But she knew a conversation with Hirutu was impossible so she bowed and said, "I thank you for this opportunity, my grandfather."

The following day she packed her small bag. Mirako accompanied her to the airport and together they travelled to Sapporo on the island of Hokkaido. On arrival, they boarded a bus and travelled towards the mountains of Shimukappu. It was a 2.5-hour journey, and Sakura was in awe of the scenery. They travelled across valleys and over snow-covered mountains.

Sakura had never felt so isolated. She was in a foreign country far from home. Whilst Mirako was comforting her, she could only ponder what her life would be like in the future. They exited the bus at a barren open area containing a single structure, a snow-covered shed in a solitary valley at the base of a mountain. She was cold, her clothing insufficient after leaving the heated bus.

Mirako put her arm around her and together they waited. Sakura felt miserable and suspected Mirako would have preferred to be back home as well. She kept talking to her, asking her to be patient and telling her Hirutu knew this path was correct for her. The snowfall became heavier and Sakura wondered if she would die here, the icy damp air chilling her bones.

Ghost-like characters appeared through the veil of snow and two monks and four horses emerged from the blanket of white. They bowed and presented Sakura and Mirako with two thick coats to wear. The coats were made from llama wool and initially felt cold against her body; however, the yarn quickly started to warm her. They helped her mount a horse then they all rode off into the snow.

***

They arrived at the Temple at night and were escorted to a room containing two tatami mats and a small table in the corner. Exhausted, sleep came quickly.

Sakura awoke with the sun shining through a high window and examined the room. The walls were constructed from stone blocks, each approximately 30 cm tall and 60 cm wide. The room was rudimentary yet spacious, three metres by three metres. The door was wooden with solid brass fittings. It looked ancient, possibly built centuries ago. The room retained a fragrance of spice and musk, the residue from burnt incense and the scent from the bodies which had shared this room.

Mirako began to stir. "Good morning," said Sakura. Mirako smiled, "Your new life starts here today, Sakura. Master Shi Yan Ming is the greatest Sohei monk in Japan. The Sohei monks are 'warrior monks', and he will teach you many fighting skills and the philosophy of the Sohei. The training will refocus your mind, remove past trauma and provide you with skills and knowledge to live a fulfilling life."

Sakura was glad Mirako was here and asked her, "How long will you stay with me?"

"Sakura, this journey is yours. I cannot stay here with you. I will leave today after we meet Master Shi Yan Ming. I will return for your 12th birthday to see how you have grown."

There was a knock at the door. A monk asked them to follow him and they walked along a cold, damp stone corridor into a large warm room. Fires were burning in four large stone hearths along the two opposing walls. It was an eating hall and it was breakfast time, the tables occupied by the temple monks enjoying their morning meal.

Breakfast was a simple rice porridge with fish and vegetables. Afterwards, the monk who had escorted them from their room came over, bowed and said, "I will take you to meet Master Shi Yan Ming."

Master Ming was an elderly, sinewy man who appeared to be in his seventies. His hair was wispy and greying, accompanied by an exiguous goatee beard, whitened from age. Whilst short in stature, he projected an aura of confidence that made him both mysterious and intimidating at the same time. He stared at Sakura. Mirako put her arm around Sakura and encouraged her to move forward and bow before him.

Master Ming said, "Sakura, your grandfather has asked me to care for you. I respect his wishes, yet that does not mean your life will be easy for you here. If you train well and respect your teachers, you will endure. If not......Well let's just say that I don't want to have that conversation with Hirutu."

Sakura didn't know it then but that was the beginning of almost a decade of training in the Sohei temple. How had her life changed so quickly?

Nine

Sakura had discovered the temple was built in 1455 and had protected generations of monks over the centuries. Her morning started at 5:00am with the great bell ringing in the courtyard. She would get dressed in her unadorned course llama hair robe, empty her chamber pot and then eat a simple breakfast followed by thirty minutes of meditation.

At 6:30am she commenced her temple chore carrying water from the ancient well in the courtyard and filling one of the kitchen water storage vats. These vats were used for cooking and dishwashing throughout the day and held 200 litres of water. It took 20 journeys to replenish the vat, carrying two five-litre stone jugs suspended across her back on a bamboo rod. At first, this wasn't easy and she could only half-fill the jugs requiring 40 journeys. Over time she became more robust and after five months she was ready to start carrying larger vessels, each holding 10 litres.

After completing their chores, the young monks trained together undertaking different exercises and challenges set by their teachers to harden their bodies.

After lunch there was an hour of scripture and history training. Sakura enjoyed learning about the past and how the Sohei monks had prospered. They told stories of famous monk warriors, their battle strategies and how they defended the temple. They also taught the importance of balance through nature, mind and body.

In the afternoon her favourite daily activity was martial arts training which took place over three hours. She was duelling with boys her age now as few females were in training and she had surpassed their competency.

After training she was allowed 30 mins of free time and would walk the gardens or spend time with others. She enjoyed talking to the elder monks and learning from their wisdom.

Once a year each student was allowed one visitation, a maximum of two people, and could send and receive one letter. Sakura had decided she would write a letter each year to Natasha to tell her how she was progressing. The nurse had become like a mother to her during her recovery. Her grandmother and grandfather could visit her at the temple for her annual visit. One night, about a month into her training, she sat at her small table in the corner of the room and wrote her first letter.

Dear Natasha,

I hope this letter finds you well.
I miss you.
My grandparents have been very kind. Their home and gardens are spectacular. I am enjoying the experience of being in Japan.

I have begun training to become a Sohei Warrior. It is an incredible honour to be accepted by the temple. I am grateful for the wide-reaching influence of my grandfather which has enabled me to undertake this internship.

I live in the mountains in an ancient temple and the work and training are challenging yet fulfilling. The monks possess knowledge and insights which they share. I have learnt so much already that I cannot fathom what I will know at the end of my training.

Access to the outside world is restricted to ensure we are focused entirely on our training. I am allowed to receive and write one letter a year. I intend to write to you every year to tell you about my journey and how I am healing. I have already noticed improvements in my body and mind from the discipline of exercise and our rudimentary diet.

I am hoping you can write to me. It will be a peculiar conversation as the letters are sent and collected from the post office once a year. Our letters could be up to a year old when we receive them. I have written the address at the bottom of this letter.

Love Sakura.

My address is: -
Student Sakura Bianchi
Sohei Temple
Shimukappu
Island of Hokkaido
Japan

After six months, Sakura started to have dreams, no.... not dreams, nightmares of that terrible night. Perhaps the meditation and training had bolstered her mind, preparing her to cope with the memories.

At first, the dreams were confusing. The scenes were concealed, like peering through a thick fog. However, over the next three months, the visions revealed more. It was the face masks that manifested first. There were five home invaders, all of them wearing ridiculous masks. Sakura could remember all the masks - four animal characters, a wolf, a duck, a mouse, a pig and the last was a weird-looking face stretched out of proportion. She had named this character 'Goofy'.

In the dream, an enormous man wearing a wolf mask was on top of her. He was hurting her and she was screaming for him to stop. There was a moment when he loosened his grip on her right arm allowing her to reach up and pull the wolf mask away.

The face she saw was pure evil and now that she remembered, it would stay with her forever. The eyes were a deep blue with heavily hooded brows, his black hair thick with a curl, a bead of sweat about to drip from it. A massive fist crashed into her jaw, shattering it. The pain was incredible. Sparks flashed before her eyes and then nothing as she lost consciousness.

The dream became more frequent. Her mind was forcing her to remember. She now thought of this man as the big bad wolf. She had made him a fictitious character and in a small way this lessened the hurt. It encouraged her to remember more.

One night she dreamed of a time with her mother, they had just watched a movie at Bexley cinema and had stopped for petrol. As they entered the service station, she could see the glow of the neon lights against the setting sun. They spelt out 7-Eleven.

Her mother filled the car and said, "Sakura, go and select a chocolate bar." "Ok, Mummy." Sakura walked briskly into the service station towards the shelf containing a vast selection of chocolates. She stood in awe, so many choices! Which should she choose? The man behind the counter walked towards her and stood beside her. He placed one enormous hand on her shoulder and pointed at a Cherry Ripe chocolate bar with the other. She had never eaten a Cherry Ripe before.

He said, "These are two for one so your mother can have one too." He took two bars from the shelf for her. While speaking, his hand slid slowly down her back, travelling like a serpent down her spine, finishing its journey on her bottom, which he squeezed. His touch was unwelcome; she stiffened and felt afraid. The doors opened, her mother entered, and the man released her. She could read the badge on his shirt, *Roy*. She knew this was the man in the wolf mask.

Sakura awoke from the dream, her heart racing, her body saturated with sweat, yet she felt cold and clammy with the name *Roy, Roy, Roy* repeating in her mind.

Despite her small room being in absolute darkness, she could easily navigate to her reading table in the corner. She sat crossed legged on the cushion under the table, reached for the matchbox and turned her head away as she struck a match. The flare of the match illuminated the room instantly and then it dimmed as the flame on the match settled. She put the match to the candle wick and watched it ignite, then extinguished the match and placed it in an old stone bowl with two of its partners. As the candle began to burn brighter, the reading table was cast in that beautiful yellow orb only a wax candle can create. She opened the notebook her grandmother had given her to record memories of her life at the temple, put pen to paper and wrote.

The big bad wolf is Roy. He works at the 7-Eleven service station in or near Bexley.'

Satisfied she would remember the dream's meaning when she awoke in the morning, Sakura blew out the candle and returned to bed. As she pulled the llama wool blanket over her, she could smell the hint of the beast that had provided the wool, a pleasant calming scent. Her bed started to warm up and she felt peaceful in this safe nest within these solid stone walls erected centuries ago. She felt elated, the feeling you get when placing the last piece of a jigsaw puzzle, standing back and admiring what you have achieved. Roy was that jigsaw piece. She knew her grandfather could track him down and once they had Roy, he would tell them the names of the other four men. She drifted off to sleep feeling cheerful, perhaps the happiest she felt since waking from her coma in the hospital.

***

On her 12th birthday, she was pleasantly surprised to see Mirako. She had travelled from Tokyo to visit her for a couple of days. Master Shi Yan Ming had provided his blessing that Sakura could travel to the local village of Shimukappu with Mirako. It was Spring and a beautiful time of the year, her favourite season. The cherry blossoms were in flower, turning the village into a wonderland.

Mirako asked, "Sakura, do you remember anything from the night of your mother's death?"

Sakura smiled and said, "I have remembered!" She spent the next 10 minutes explaining the nightmares, the masks and that she had seen the face of one of the men. She was sure his name was Roy and he worked at the Bexley 7-Eleven service station. She provided Roy's description to Mirako.

Mirako said, "Well done, Sakura. I will discuss this with Hirutu and we will find this man. You will have your chance to see him again and avenge your mother."

"Mirako, in my dream, this man is hurting me in my private place. Did they do bad things to me?"

Mirako's eyes grew glassy and there was a long pause before she said, "Sakura, when you are ready, your grandfather and I will tell you everything we know about what happened on that dreadful night. Until then, it is best to focus on your training, knowing it will allow you to get justice for yourself and your mother."

They spent two days together visiting the various stores and cafes in the small village. Sakura enjoyed the variety of food which differed considerably from her regular temple diet.

The monks arrived to return Sakura and the spare horse which Mirako had ridden to the Sohei Temple. Sakura felt sad when she farewelled her grandmother. She had cherished their time together.

Ten

Hirutu said goodbye to Mirako, placed the telephone handset back into the cradle and smiled. His first smile in over a year, the first since his daughter's murder and the brutalisation of his granddaughter.

At last they had a name and a description.

He immediately dispatched two of his best men to Australia to search for the man Sakura had described. They would locate him or commit seppuku if they failed. He had requested Mirako to stay longer in the village of Shimukappu whilst they searched for this Roy.

It had only taken three days since his men left Tokyo until Hirutu received the photograph. His name was Roy Homer and the photo matched Sakura's description. He emailed the picture to Mirako and then called her, requesting she travel back to the Sohei Temple to show the image to Sakura and verify if this was the man.

It took Mirako a day of travelling the mountain trails to reach the temple. She had secured a horse from the village and undertaken the arduous journey alone. The deep valleys and steep-sided mountains had protected the Temple location for centuries and still achieved that today.

She was exhausted when she arrived. She was 56 years of age this year, much too old to endure this journey, but this was for Sakura and Aiko (her only daughter). She was heartbroken, angry and wished she had disobeyed her beloved husband and visited Aiko in Australia. She should have been there for her granddaughter's birth but her husband's pride prohibited it.

It was a cold February day when Aiko told them she was in love with Enzo Bianchi, a handsome Italian man. When she asked their permission to marry, Hirutu became enraged. How dare Aiko discontinue their Japanese bloodline by mixing it with an Italian! He had stormed from the room. Mirako had never seen him so angry and she was afraid for Enzo and Aiko. She told them they must flee Japan immediately. Her husband was a dangerous and powerful man who had accumulated immense wealth over his lifetime whilst leading the Hotato Yakuza. His wealth and position provided him the freedom to kill anyone. That day was the last contact she had with Aiko.

Mirako met Sakura in the garden during her afternoon free time. She showed her the photo Hirutu's men had taken in Australia. Sakura confirmed that it was the man in her nightmares. She was positive he was one of the men there that night. Mirako rested that night in Sakura's room, preparing her mind and body for the journey back to the village where she would contact Hirutu and then fly back to Tokyo.

Her husband's influence had allowed Mirako this second visit in a single year, the proviso being that there would be no visit in the subsequent year. While this was a painful compromise, the confirmation that they had the correct man would make the sacrifice worthwhile.

***

Once Hirutu received confirmation from his wife, he contacted his men and confirmed they had found the correct man. He thanked them for their diligence. Next, he wanted them to locate a reliable and discreet man to maintain surveillance over Roy Homer. This man would email Hirutu monthly updates outlining Roy's activities, including where he lived and worked. He would be paid handsomely for each report.

Hirutu would wait until Sakura was older and more powerful. He would allow her the opportunity to achieve their family justice. He knew this would be necessary for Sakura's well-being and it would allow her to recover from the trauma of her ordeal.

Eleven

Sakura had been at the temple for four years and she had started to develop into a woman. Her breasts had grown and whilst not large, they were noticeable under her robe. She knew this from the way the boys looked at her.

Her body had hardened from the training and her arms were tanned and corded with muscle. Her waist and hips had developed into that iconic hourglass figure denoting a woman, terminating in slender yet shapely legs. Her Eurasian features, a mixture of her Japanese mother and Italian father, gave her an exotic appearance. The only blemish was a small scar on her jaw resulting from a crushing blow she incurred the night they had been attacked.

She always trained hard and today was the first time she punched her hand through the bamboo board. Master Ming applauded when she split the bamboo. She had achieved this using the 2 finger strike, a brutal strike using just the first two fingers. Years of practice had transformed the bones in her hands. Now they were as hard as steel. She could strike with speed and power and today she had succeeded. She was becoming a warrior monk.

Sakura was excited. Tomorrow was her 15th birthday and she hoped to see Mirako who visited on her birthday most years. Yes, today was a good day. She couldn't wait to tell Mirako of her achievement.

Part 3

Present Day

Roy's Justice

Twelve

Once Sakura had entered Roy's house, she commenced her preparations. First, she removed the restraints from her backpack and attached them to the bed. He was a strong man but not strong enough to break through these.

She removed the vial of Oleandrin that she had prepared this week. She had extracted the Oleandrin from the beautiful Oleander tree known for its striking flowers and commonly grown in Australia. The Ancient Romans were the first to discover that the Oleander tree contained a lethal cardiac glycoside known as Oleandrin. Indeed, the toxins in Oleander are so potent that people have become ill after eating honey made by bees that visit the flowers. Sakura's training included how to extract the toxin to induce paralysis.

She prepared the dart by carefully sucking on the end to create a vacuum, saturating the dart tip with the toxin. She placed the dart next to the blowgun and opened the backpack to remove the special surprise she had for Roy. The surprise was a creation of her own, something she thought worthy for this man who liked to hurt little girls and women with his oversized penis. She prepared this last week by soaking a cotton thread in an accelerant, blending it with aluminium and magnesium particles and adding potassium nitrate as the oxidant. Finally, the cord was covered in a thin layer of wax to seal it. This combination of minerals and chemicals gave the thread unique combustible qualities. Once lit it would burn at extreme temperatures. The magnesium made it inextinguishable and it would burn even underwater.

She had threaded it through a hollow wooden tube, 250mm long and 3mm in diameter leaving 10 centimetres exposed at the top of the tube. The other end, a metre long, once through the tube had been carefully wound around the tube, starting at the base and finishing at the top. When lit, the cord would act like a wick burning down through the centre of the tube, igniting the coils on the outside and burning from the bottom to the top of the tube. It would burn slowly up the outside of the tube, incinerating itself and leaving little evidence of its existence. She placed her surprise on the bedside table along with her other instruments of torture.

She had finished her preparations by 6:45pm and meditated while she waited. She exited her meditation when she heard the car. She watched him enter the kitchen and disarm the house security. She was ready. Her heartbeat quickened. Finally, this day had come.

She watched him make a drink and when his head was at the correct angle, she placed the dart in the blowgun, steadied her mind, took a breath, aimed, and blew. A hit and almost instantly Roy became unsteady on his feet. Sakura walked towards him. He couldn't see her; his eyes had turned upwards, back into his head. She prevented him from smashing his head on the floor, as he passed out, by catching his shoulders and lowering him to the floor. She opened his left eyelid to assess her handiwork, hoping the dose of the toxin wasn't excessive. She didn't want him to die, well, not yet. Roy knew who the other men were; the mission would fail if he were to die before she interrogated him.

It had been an effort to drag him into the bedroom and onto the bed. He was a lot heavier than her. She knew that once he was awake he would deny his involvement. What an idiot.

He cried like a baby when she removed his right testicle, then, in an effort to preserve his remaining testicle he had revealed the other offenders. She recorded the entire confession, why they did it, who wore which mask, their names and addresses. When he had finished his testimonial she asked him if he was thirsty and he thanked her.

She gave him a 500ml bottle of water, which she had laced with Bumetanide, a powerful diuretic and 300mg of Viagra. Roy drank it all down. When he had finished drinking, she removed the bottle from his mouth and quickly placed a special mouth guard in his mouth, anchoring its strap around his head.

She had fabricated this mouthguard last week. It was a wooden ball with a hole in the middle that fitted the spout she would screw onto the bottle. The mouthpiece was held in place by an elastic strap around his head. The wooden ball filled his mouth cavity making it difficult for him to talk. She attached the plastic spout to the drink bottle and refilled it from the wine cask she had carried in her backpack. She included some of Roy's Makers Mark. If he liked Bourbon, why not?

Roy was terrified. He had never felt fear like this before. It permeated his body, every pore, every nerve; he wanted to cry. He was ashamed that he had wept during the interrogation. This bitch had cut off his testicle and waved it before his eyes like a war trophy. He had told her everything. He wanted her to go, to leave him alone. He had been thirsty and now she had stuck something in his mouth and secured it behind his immobilised head. He couldn't spit it out. "Fuck you, fuck you, bitch!" he tried to say, but the mouth guard transformed the words into an incoherent mumble.

She held a plastic bottle containing a red liquid. It had a straw-like spout that fit perfectly into the hole in the ball she was using to keep his mouth open. She started to pour. It burned. It tasted like Bourbon and wine and he tried not to swallow it. Then she pinched his nose closed. She said, "Drink, Roy, and I will let you breathe."

So he drank. Finally, it was over, the bottle empty. The woman asked him if he would like another. He would shake his head if he could. He would say no if he could. The best he could do was grunt.

Sakura looked at her watch. It was 9:00pm and she was on track to commence the next part of her plan. She sat on the bed and leaned over

42

so he could see her. She took hold of his penis and stimulated him as she whispered, "Roy did you enjoy destroying a little girl's innocence?" Despite losing a testicle, the 300mg of Viagra was sufficient to arouse Roy to a full erection.

Sakura applied Vaseline to one end of Roy's surprise. Using two fingers of her gloved hand she spread open the eye of his penis and with the other, she proceeded to push the 250mm long device into Roy's urethra. At first there was resistance to the sizeable tube but once it did go inside, she could push it the entire length. Only the wick emerged from his penis. She gave a little giggle. It's Roy's penis candle.

Roy knew she was doing something to him, but because he couldn't move his head, he couldn't see. The bitch was interfering with his manhood. She had inserted something inside his penis and it hurt.

She returned to his vision and looked down at him. He studied her face noticing the absence of emotion. Her eyes were dark and menacing. In his inebriated and aroused state he realised she was beautiful. He also admitted he was terrified. His heart was pounding, attempting to break through his chest and escape.

She said, "Roy, this is my gift for what you did to me and my mummy." She flicked the wheel of a cigarette lighter and ignited the wick, which burnt slowly down the inside of the wooden tube. A column of smoke ascended from his penis. When it reached the bottom of the tube, 250mm inside Roy's body, he reacted violently to the sudden intense pain—his body arched and strained against the restraints, but they held. Roy's screaming was muffled by the mouthguard. Sakura could hear the hiss of steam as blood vessels and flesh were scorched and evaporated by the heat. The magnesium in the cord burnt at 2000C, an unstoppable chemical reaction and she knew the pain must be excruciating.

The intensity of the light from the combustion illuminated his penis. Sakura could see the flame journey upwards through his now transparent penis as it cauterised his urethra, destroying the penile structures.

It was over in a few minutes and Roy slumped back onto the bed, his brow beaded with sweat, his face glowing red. Roy's once proud manhood now withered and dried, the head of his penis charred and sealed shut. Roy struggled to free himself, his face a twisted mask of pain and terror, the pain from his expanded bladder and burnt penis clearly showing on his face.

Unfortunately for Roy, this wasn't the end of his ordeal.

Sakura leaned over him so he could see her face and asked if he would enjoy another drink. She placed another bottle of wine into the mouth guard and forced him to drink by holding his nose closed.

After 15 minutes, his stomach was grossly extended, allowing his bladder to stretch to a size well beyond its design limits. Sakura pressed her finger into his stomach, he shuddered and tears streamed from his eyes. She could feel his bladder and it was enormous.

She smiled at him. He was frantic. She entertained herself over the next 10 minutes pushing deeply upon his stomach, watching him shudder with each touch, his movement restricted by the restraints. Finally, satisfied he had suffered sufficiently, she positioned herself so he could see her face. Smiling she said, "So Roy, how does it feel to be completely helpless and in pain? I spent months in hospital recovering from the injuries you and the others inflicted on me that night."

Her tongue ran across her bottom lip the moment before she struck him using the two-finger punch. The strike was brutal, her technique flawless, developed from years of training at the Sohei Temple. At first, his bladder compressed away from the strike but the urine volume was excessive and it ruptured, dumping its contents into his peritoneal cavity. The sudden release of urine pressed against his lungs forcing him to exhale. Before he could take another breath, Sakura blocked the hole in the wooden ball in his mouth with one hand and pinched his nostrils closed with the other.

She watched as his eyes expanded, full of fear. He knew his time was over but she refused to let him breathe and maintained her deadly embrace for a further five minutes.

When Sakura finally released him a feeling of euphoria descended upon her. It had been a good night. She had the names of the other perpetrators and a testicle; a memento to remember her dear old Roy. She removed a jar from her backpack and dropped the testicle into the solution of Dimethyl hydantoin, a chemical to preserve the DNA. The jar had a label with '*Mr Wolf*' written neatly in ink.

She released the restraints and cleaned the area, carefully removing any evidence of her presence. Lastly, she took a bottle of accelerant from her backpack and poured it onto the bed, over Roy and around the room. Next, she lit an incense cone and carefully placed it on the fluid-soaked sheet. The incense would burn down over 20 minutes, providing time for her to make her departure.

Thirteen

Sakura left Roy's place and returned to the car park. It was 11:00pm. She felt.... happy, relieved. She had prepared half her life for today and now had four other names. It felt very satisfying to have completed the first of five assassinations.

Well, not an assassination. She had tortured a man and felt no regret. He had imposed pain on her, her mother and many women. The world was a better place without him—a first step in her journey for recovery and justice.

She put on her helmet, placed the key in the ignition, turned it, waited till the instrument lights settled then pushed the starter. Immediately the Ducati Monster fired up, the deep sound of the pipes echoing off the concrete walls of the car park. She loved that sound. She mounted the bike, twisted the throttle and rode home.

Upon her return, she switched on her MacBook, reached under the desk to remove the USB stick from its secret hiding space and inserted it into the Mac. She loaded her Ango-Ka app from the USB. Her grandfather provided the software; his organisation used the app to send messages. It had a 512-digit encryption key which was unbreakable even with a modern supercomputer.

She took out her phone and played the recording of Roy's interrogation. The session had taken over 30 minutes and during that time, he had named each of the men who were there that night, including their ages. She had him spell their names and addresses to ensure no mistakes. She also had him describe each man's physical appearance. Roy didn't know the address of two men, just that one lived in Cairns and the other in Darwin. She saved the recording in the Ango-Ka app and sent it to her grandfather.

She included a message indicating the order in which she would dispatch the remaining men. She would use the next two weeks to observe the two Sydney targets to determine the best time and location for her attack. She requested assistance in locating the Cairns and Darwin assailants.

Next, she removed Roy's testicle from the jar, sliced a thin section, and returned the testicle to the container; its new home. She put the specimen into a small plastic Ziplock bag, sealed it and placed the Ziplock bag into one of the thick, liquid-proof postage-paid envelopes her grandfather had supplied. The envelope had been pre-addressed to the Tokyo DNA Clinic, with 'Biological Specimen Enclosed' stamped across the bottom right corner.

Sakura walked into the kitchen and made herself a pot of green tea. She carried the teapot and teacup into the lounge room, placed the delicate Japanese porcelain upon her Japanese tea ceremony table and sat cross-legged on the tatami mat. Whilst the tea brewed, she reflected on the day.

She was relieved that she had convinced Roy to reveal the name of the man who had killed her mother and the name of the man who had stabbed her. Her grandfather would commence the search for them once he received her message.

***

The next day Sakura went to have her first tattoo. She had decided on a small ribbon to straddle the scar that ran from the base of her neck to her belly button. A lovely pink tattoo, a symbol to remind her of the pain of losing her mother and her suffering during her recovery. She planned for five ribbons, one for each man she killed.

The tattooist completed the design in under 40 minutes and Sakura spent a few minutes admiring his work in the mirror. It was perfect, a pink ribbon 10 cm long, neatly positioned over the scar from the lifesaving surgery she had undergone to repair the damage from three stab wounds. She was keen to get another tattoo, and that would happen soon.

Phillip Longtree, aka Mr Duck, would be her next victim. He would pay for sodomising her.

Fourteen

Tom's first autopsy case was a victim of a suspicious house fire. He started the recorder and commenced the autopsy.

"Date is 19th January 2021; a deceased male early thirties, delivered to the morgue on 18th January 2021. The body is immolated, with extensive damage to all external structures. All phalanges are missing except for the right-hand thumb.

There is extensive damage to the legs, including loss of all flesh from the feet, and over 90% of the gluteus maximus have been incinerated due to their high-fat content."

Tom made the classic autopsy y-incision from shoulder to shoulder, meeting at the breastbone and then down to the pubic bone.

"I am opening the chest cavity. I can see that the bladder has ruptured filling the peritoneal cavity with urine."

Now that is interesting!

In 35 years of conducting autopsies, Tom had only seen one ruptured bladder, a victim of a high-speed motor vehicle accident. The toxicologist report stated the deceased had consumed a large quantity of red wine and Bourbon and a combination of Viagra and Bumetanide (a potent diuretic) before death. The alcohol and Bumetanide would have produced significant volumes of urine.

So why wasn't this expelled from the bladder?

What had prevented the egress?
He continued the recording.

"There is significant burn damage to the genitals, little remains of the penis, and the right testicle has been incinerated completely with fire damage within the scrotum. The other testicle is intact, charred and shrunken. Only a short 2cm section of the penis remains; the rest burnt away in the fire. Visual examination reveals the urethra is sealed closed. I am making an incision through the penis to the y-incision. The urethra is cauterised well into the body, much further than I expected."

Tom began examining the urinary tract starting at the bladder and working his way to where the urethra exited the penis. He was searching for a blockage; perhaps a kidney stone had prevented the victim from urinating. He wondered how the deceased could have slept through the pain of his bladder filling to a size that resulted in rupture. Even inebriated, it would have been excruciating. He took tissue samples for forensics.

He continued, "The cause of death is asphyxiation unrelated to the fire. There is no evidence of smoke inhalation in the victim's lungs, indicating he was dead before the fire started."

He stopped the recording.

He was sure this was no accidental death. He removed his scrubs and left the morgue to contact the Chief of Police and advise him of a homicide.

Fifteen

Detective Peter Reynolds had been summoned to the chief's office. He suspected another case would be assigned to him on top of his already overloaded work files.

He knocked on the door and walked in, "Hi, Chief, what's up?"

"Sit down, Peter. There was a fire at 15 Holbrook St Bexley South. It initially appeared to be accidental. The deceased was drunk and probably smoking in bed. However, the medical examiner found discrepancies during the autopsy. I want you to investigate and have your draft report on my desk in 2 days. You can take Kim Lewis as your support."

Reynolds and Lewis decided to meet first with the medical examiner. He rang Tom and arranged to meet him during his lunch break at 1:00pm. They met in the cafe on a nearby corner of the office. Peter ordered a hamburger with the lot and a Coke to wash it down. Tom ordered a salad sandwich, and Kim Lewis just had a coffee for lunch. He was on a diet and aimed to lose 10kg. He started weight loss earlier this month, and Peter thought Kim's face was thinner.

Tom started the conversation, "Most injuries were consistent for a burn victim except for two specific areas. His penis had burnt away; however, I managed to examine the remaining section and discovered the urethra had been cauterised along the length of the penis and a further 5cm into the body. I have never seen this in a burn victim before.

The urethra is a tubular organ for dispensing urine from the bladder and is very moist tissue, making it difficult to burn. For it to be cauterised like it was and so deep into the body, I suspect something hot had been inserted into the penis. There were particles of magnesium and accelerants present in the tissue.

Also, the bladder had enlarged due to diuretics and alcohol. Because of the sealed urinary tract, urine could not discharge and the bladder had expanded beyond its maximum. What should have occurred was for the urine to start backing up into the kidneys; instead, the bladder ruptured. It would take an extraordinary amount of force to do that."

Peter said, "Like a punch or a kick?"

"Maybe, if a professional boxer or MMA fighter delivered it. Also, the victim didn't have any smoke in his lungs, meaning he was dead before the fire commenced."

Tom continued, "I believe the victim was tortured before being suffocated. The fire was lit solely to erase evidence from the homicide scene and obscure the injuries. Luckily the fire brigade arrived quickly and extinguished the fire before all the evidence was destroyed."

Peter and Kim thanked Tom for his time and asked if he could provide a sample for the DNA Crimes Database to check against previous crimes. They travelled to Roy's house to investigate the crime scene and interview the neighbours.

During the remainder of the day, they interviewed 50 residents, everyone who lived in the immediate area. No one had seen anything out of the ordinary that night. Well, except when the fire blew out the bedroom window, the nearest neighbour had rung the fire brigade.

It was 6:00pm when they returned to the office to review Roy's police records. They discovered that Roy had an extensive criminal past stretching back to the juvenile years. He had been charged with carnal knowledge of three girls, all under 13 years of age, when he was 14. He had been in court for assault on multiple occasions and aggravated sexual assault by five women over the past three years.

The next day was Roy's funeral. They would attend. Perhaps a mourner could provide a lead on a potential suspect.

Sixteen

Hirutu gently touched the spacebar on his laptop to stop the playback of Roy's interrogation. He was smiling. It was the second time he had listened to the recording. He reviewed it against his written notes this time.

Sakura had demonstrated she was a skillful interrogator, obtaining all the information required to locate the remaining four perpetrators. These men would pay dearly for what they did that night.

He looked at his watch and performed a quick calculation. It was 1:00am in Tokyo, which made it 3:00am in Sydney. Excellent. He should be able to obtain the necessary information within the next 12 hours.

During the past year he had identified people in Australia who held influential positions in multiple industries. He would use these people to enable him to obtain valuable information for their cause. The Yakuza knew that every man and woman had a weakness, and weaknesses could provide leverage. He was able to influence some of the contacts with money and others with blackmail.

The Yakuza had many tentacles, and he utilised another Yakuza family in Australia to organise these connections. He wasn't sure what the future commitment to the Yakuza would be for their service but knew he would have to repay the obligation.

Regardless, it was worthwhile and he had no regrets. He opened the Gmail app on his laptop. He had 20 alternative email addresses assigned to him, reserved for temporary discussions such as this one. His technicians had created these ensuring the accounts were untraceable.

His office internet connection alternated between multiple private VPNs bouncing across 30 ISPs across the globe. The last VPN was very special and before sending the email to the recipient it would erase the previous three VPN tunnels, effectively destroying the trace information.

He opened his contacts and reviewed the list until he came across Linda Dewar, Head of the Tax Avoidance Taskforce. This position provided her with access to every Australian's tax information. He started to draft the email to the private address she had given him months earlier.

Dear Linda,

I know you will remember our phone conversation from several months ago when you agreed to provide me with specific Tax records for individuals in whom I am interested.

I require their entire history for every working year to date. I have provided their current location, so I request information for all persons with that name within 100 km of that location.

I require this information before noon today. Once I have confirmed that the data is suitable for my purpose, I will destroy the photos I have of you which would compromise your employment, and you will have no further commitments to me.

Mark Chisholm - Cairns Region

Alex Webster - Darwin

Required information: Date of Birth, Employer, Work location, Taxable income, and Residential addresses for each year's tax submissions.

Regards xxx

He hit send and then walked upstairs to his bed.

He slept till 8:00am, got up and dressed in his workout gear, had a glass of water and walked downstairs to his lounge room. His personal trainer arrived at 8:30am and they spent 60 minutes in his home gym doing cardio and weight training. After the gruelling session, he showered, dressed in casual attire, a pair of lightweight chinos, a striped polo shirt and soft leather loafers. He strolled to the balcony where breakfast was served at 10:00am.

Breakfast consisted of fruit juice, brewed coffee, Congee soup with seafood and a vegetable omelette. His wife joined him when he was finishing his omelette.

"Good morning, darling," he said as Mirako kissed him.

"How are the preparations in Australia?"

He smiled and said, "Very good. Sakura has managed to obtain all the names with sufficient information for us to complete the task."

"That's great. I look eagerly to the day Sakura avenges her mother."

"We have names and addresses for two more scumbags and I should have addresses for the others in the next hour. I expect Sakura can complete the mission within three weeks."

Mirako smiled and said, "That is good news. Sakura needs this. I need this, and you need this. I will only be satisfied when these men are punished for their sadistic sins. We will deliver them to God and he can deal with them as he sees fit."

After breakfast, Hirutu went to his study and opened his laptop. His Gmail client highlighted three emails as new, his heartbeat increased, and his breathing became shallow as he opened the email from Linda Dewar. There was no text, just two Excel files. He opened the first; it was titled Mark Chisholm. There were twenty Mark Chisholms living in the Cairns region. Hirutu knew that Mark was between 29 - 32 years of age. He could have provided Linda with the information but he wanted a comprehensive list as a precaution in case she contacted the authorities. An extensive list would stretch police resources, making maintaining 24-hour surveillance of all the men difficult.

He searched the spreadsheet's DOB column and found five men aged 29 - 32. He reviewed the individual files looking for a man who had started working in the Revesby/Bexley area and this reduced the list to just one man.

He opened his Ango-Ka app and sent the name, address and Roy's description of Mark Chisholm to Takeo. Takeo would find and follow

Mark Chisholm and determine an approach for Sakura to exact her revenge.

He repeated the same process with the Alex Webster Excel file and ended up with three potential candidates. It would be a bit more difficult for Tatsuo as he would need to eliminate two men from the suspect list.

Hopefully, Roy's description of Alex Webster would enable him to identify the person responsible. If not, then two innocent men might have to be sacrificed which was not ideal but necessary. He forwarded the information to Tatsuo then closed his laptop.

He trusted Takeo and Tatsuo with his life and knew they would work tirelessly to identify and track their targets until Sakura arrived. They would debrief her on what they had learnt about the men's behaviour and discuss scenarios they had prepared for dealing with these men.

Seventeen

Three days previously, two of Hirutu Hotato's men, Takeo Kobayashi and Tatsuo Ishikawa, had arrived in Sydney. These were Hirutu's most trusted men; both had entered Australia using false passports. They were in Australia to clean up a loose end and to aid Sakura if required.

Takeo Kobayashi was gigantic for a Japanese man standing over 200 cm tall and weighing 105kg, all muscle. A scar ran from his right ear lobe to just below his jaw, an old wound from a knife fight with two older and larger men when he was a young man of 14 years of age. He had put both men in hospital for two weeks.

News of this altercation had reached Hirutu Hotato who was always looking for recruits to join his Yakuza family. He had taken a liking to Takeo (which means 'Warrior' in Japanese) and arranged for him to be trained in multiple disciplines. Takeo had become a trusted guard over his twenty years in Hirutu Hotato's employment.

The second man, Tatsuo Ishikawa, had joined Hirutu at the beginning of his Yakuza career, and they had been friends for over 40 years. Tatsuo was of average height for a Japanese man and very powerful, resulting from a daily training regime. He had broad shoulders, a thick neck and a barrel chest. Despite being in his early sixties, he was still a formidable warrior and many younger men would think twice before confronting him.

Tatsuo meant 'Dragon Man' in Japanese, and when Sakura first met

Tatsuo at her grandfather's home, she thought 'Dragon Man' was a suitable name for him. Colourful Yakuza-style tattoos covered his entire body except his head, neck and hands. His tattooist had applied the designs using the traditional Japanese Tebori method, where a sharp piece of bamboo is dipped in ink and repeatedly pushed into the skin.

The men had spent the past two days observing Richard Chaplin's movements, searching his home and determining their approach to closing his account with Hirutu. Richard was a private investigator and had started his career in the police force. The temptation to accept bribes and protection money to supplement his low constable salary was eventually discovered. He had been lucky to avoid jail. At the time, the chief of police had preferred to avoid the negative press resulting from a police corruption story and decided to have him dismissed from the force without a conviction.

Tatsuo and Takeo met Richard nine years earlier when they were in Australia searching for the man Sakura had remembered in a dream. That man was Roy Homer and they had engaged Richard for his investigative services. The agreement was for Richard to provide monthly reports to a secure Gmail address, providing data on Roy Homer's home, work address, and social activities. He would receive a payment of $1000 for each report. Hirutu had read all the 110 reports received during the years Sakura undertook her training.

Yesterday Sakura had disposed of Roy so Richard was of no more value to Hirutu and instead had become a liability. Yakuza have a saying, "When other people know your secret, it can only be truly safe when those people are dead."

Eighteen

Richard had arrived home early to complete his monthly report on Roy Homer, as he had for the past nine years. It was a profitable activity only requiring 30 minutes a week to check that Roy was still running protection, visiting the gym and validating his home address.

He had often wondered who the client was and why the interest in this man. The Japanese men who had approached him all those years ago were probably gangsters. However, they spoke fluent English with an articulation that suggested they had been well-educated. One of the men was enormous, towering over him when they entered his office. Studying their eyes, he was conscious these men demanded respect and not the sort of men you betray.

Richard wasn't the type of man to get frightened easily; however, in these mens' presence, he had felt vulnerable and almost hadn't agreed to their request. He considered their offer. He couldn't see any harm in it. They were not asking him to do anything illegal so he had agreed.

He never received a response to his emails, but every month, one or two days after he sent the report, the money would be in his account. He thought the assignment would only last a couple of months but as time passed, he relaxed and enjoyed the monthly payment.

He finished the report, sent it and went to the kitchen to mix himself a gin and tonic. Upon returning to his lounge room he heard his laptop beep, the sound of incoming mail. He opened the mail inbox and saw that his report had bounced. The mail server message; *'unknown recipient'.*

That was strange. He checked the email address spelling and it was correct. Of course it was correct. He had been using this email account for years. They must have deleted the account. Why?

He made another drink, sat on his dirty and too-soft sofa, used the remote to turn on the TV and took a long swallow. The gin and tonic tasted good, but the bounced email had unsettled him. What could it mean?

The nightly news started. The opening story and video footage were of a home fire from last night. The newsreader went on to explain that the occupant had died. The fire brigade thought it was accidental. The blaze had started in the bedroom and it appeared the deceased had been smoking in bed.

Richard lowered his glass and placed it gently on the side table. The house on the news was Roy Homer's. He had driven by the home hundreds of times and it was unmistakably his. He could feel his heart racing; his renal glands had just dumped a shot of adrenalin into him. His autonomic nervous system activated, and his body entered hyper-arousal. He was now well into 'fight or flight' mode. He tried a deep breath to calm himself and realised he was terrified. At that moment, there was a heavy knock at his front door and he almost pissed himself.

He sat still for a moment considering his options. He wasn't expecting visitors; he rarely had visitors. He also doubted the visit was coincidental. Roy was dead, the Gmail account no longer existed, and the knock at his door was probably related. He decided answering the door was not an option.

Instead, he went into his bedroom, opened the bedside table and removed the Glock 17 he kept there. One of the perks of being a Private Investigator was obtaining a concealed weapon license. He had chosen the Glock 17 as his pistol of choice for four reasons. Firstly, it was chambered for 9mm rounds which could stop a man from 20 metres. They were readily available for purchase, were relatively inexpensive and easily concealed under a jacket due to its lighter polymer frame. He practised weekly and was competent and experienced in its use. He could discharge this weapon quickly and efficiently if he needed to protect himself.

There was a second knock at the door, heavier and louder this time. Richard decided to exit the house by the rear door. He pushed the 9mm magazine firmly into the handle of the Glock, hearing it click in place and cycled the slide chambering a 9mm cartridge. He flipped the safety off and, now armed, began to feel less intimidated. He moved towards the front door and standing to the side, flicked on the light switch with an outstretched arm. The light on the verandah was directly over the front door. It was bright and he hoped it would affect the night vision of whoever was standing at the door, potentially gaining him precious seconds.

He raced towards the rear door. A quick look through the window revealed the rear porch was clear. He quietly opened the door and exited. He ran along the side path that led to the road as fast as he dared.

Tatsuo was waiting in the dark at the rear of the house; behind a bush that provided cover from anyone leaving by the rear path. He could hear the second knock on the door and shortly afterwards, the back door opening. He took a deep breath and steadied himself on the balls of his feet. He listened to the footfalls of the running man and timed his blow for the moment he ran past him.

He threw out his left arm, holding it straight and bracing for the impact. Richard ran straight into it, Tatsuo's strong forearm buried into Richard's throat, as solid as a steel beam. The gun flew from his hand and his legs maintained their forward momentum but since he was held stationary, they lifted off the path and did a peculiar air walk.

Tatsuo positioned his right forearm over Richard's forehead and, with ease, twisted his head quickly to the right breaking his neck and severing the spinal cord. Within seconds Richard was dead. He lifted him onto his right shoulder and walked out to the car where Takeo stood with the boot open. Tatsuo laid him inside the boot and they both got into the car and drove to Richard's final resting place 15 km away.

They had chosen Lake Gillawarna at Georges Hall. When they arrived,

Takeo used bolt-cutters to remove the padlock from the gate which prevented entry after dark. They had purchased the bolt cutters earlier that day along with a three-metre length of chain and four cinder concrete blocks. Lake Gillawarna was shallow, so it was vital for them to weigh the body down. Takeo carried the body and Tatsuo brought the other items to the lake's edge. They secured the concrete blocks to the body using the chain and then together, they swung him twice before letting go and casting him several metres into the lake.

Bubbles arose as he disappeared under the lily pads on his way to the shallow bottom. The lake was teeming with fish and other aquatic life. They suspected very little would remain of Richard after a week and his body might never be discovered.

They drove back to their hotel, the Four Seasons at Circular Quay, and dined on sashimi celebrating the completion of their first assignment with sake. Back in their rooms they accessed their email. Both men had a laptop and a USB Key that held the special Ango-Ka software used by their organisation to communicate secretly. Only four people had the encryption key, the others being Sakura and Hirutu.

Tatsuo read his message; it simply said, 'Your assignment is to locate Alex Webster in Darwin and monitor until further advised. See attached information.'

Takeo read his message: 'Your assignment is to locate Mark Chisholm in Cairns and monitor until further advised. See attached information.'

Both men responded with, 'Message received and understood. All loose ends dealt with in Sydney.'

Nineteen

Phillip attended Roy's funeral and sat alone in the second row of seats. They had been friends for a long time. It's funny; he always thought that friends were so important when you're young and that you would do anything for them. Then as you got older, friends became less important. Phillip had done things with Roy he would prefer to forget. Roy wasn't a nice guy. Roy was an alpha male prick.

A dozen mourners were at the funeral service, including two police officers. Phillip had watched the news reports which indicated the police were treating Roy's death as an accident. He didn't think it was an accident. Roy didn't smoke, so how did his bed catch alight?

When the service ended, the police approached him and asked him to accompany them to the station for an interview. He had waited ninety minutes before his turn and the discussion took an hour. The police had offered him a coffee but Phillip had declined as he didn't want to leave any DNA samples. He didn't leave the police station until after 6:00pm and he went straight home.

An hour later he was drinking his third beer at his kitchen table. The house was old and small. The rent took most of his pay and the rest he spent on food and alcohol. The house was on the street's high side and he liked the view from the kitchen windows. He could see the lights of Sydney when sitting at his kitchen table.

He was reflecting on the day, thinking about his shitty life. He would be 29 next month and had fuck all to show for it. He hoped he would have more than ten people attend his funeral when he died but deep down he knew it would also be a sparse turnout.

Over the years he had become more reclusive and drank heavily. He didn't have many friends. Roy was probably his best friend so there wasn't comfort in that thought. Roy was a prick and probably one of the reasons Phillip's life was so shitty.

He started to contemplate why and when his life became so monotonous, so empty. He had never been good-looking so he had to work hard to find a partner. Usually, the women he dated were the ones other men didn't want. He felt cheated which manifested in violent tendencies towards women. When they wouldn't give him what he wanted he would force them. Sometimes he was more violent than he meant to be. Violence was his tool of persuasion.

He blamed his father for his behaviour. His father was a drunken no-hoper, often out of work, mostly pissed and full of anger. Phillip was only eight years of age when his father started to beat his mother. At first, the beatings were infrequent, but soon became a weekly event. After a while, he would recognise the signals moments before his father's temper erupted, hide under his bed and cry. He was only a tiny boy and couldn't help his mother. He was pathetic.

Phillip took plenty of beatings over the years as well and his mother was unable to protect him during his father's rages. Over time he started to despise his mother for making him feel helpless and pathetic. Strangely and illogically, his anger turned towards her rather than his father. He hated his mother's inability to defend them.

As he got older and entered his teens, he struggled to control his emotions, the result of testosterone and other hormones raging through his body. He was desperate for sexual relief, his desire so intense he would do whatever it took to relieve it.

Those early years had defined him. The consequences of his actions landed him in trouble with the law, limiting his job opportunities and friends.

The awareness came quickly, like a punch in the guts, and was painful.

He had become just like his father.

Twenty

Peter parked the police cruiser at the crematorium; there were only a few other cars.

Kim said, "It shouldn't take much to cremate him; he's already half done." Peter laughed. Neither of them sympathised with Roy after reading his police report.

They regained their composure and walked towards the building with a black stretched vehicle parked at the front doors. A paper sign on the door read, *'Celebrating the life of Roy Homer'*.

They entered the building and sat in the back row as the service commenced. The room was mostly empty, apparently, only a few people wished to celebrate Roy Homer's life.

When the service ended, the curtains closed around the coffin and the mourners began to leave. Peter and Kim quickly rose and went outside, keen to interview everyone for a lead. The mourners included his parents, two brothers and a sister. Peter spoke to them and arranged to meet them at their house in the morning to ask them questions about Roy's death. Kim recorded the names of the other five mourners and asked them to come down to the station for an interview that afternoon. Several were not too happy with this request and begrudgingly agreed.

***

The first interview was with Max Dillon. He was a personal trainer at the gym and had known Roy for three years. Max was a big man, clearly a bodybuilder, and he needed a strong man to spot him because he used heavy weights. Roy also pumped heavy iron so the relationship was one of convenience rather than friendship, each man having the other to spot for them.

The second interviewee was Catherine Roberts. She also attended the gym where Roy trained and said she had come to pay her respects. Both Reynolds and Lee suspected there was more to their relationship. Still, when questioned about the friendship, she became defensive and claimed she only saw him at the gym and occasionally said hi.

Next were Wendy Stockholm and Sharon Tate. These two women had previously filed charges against Roy and it was apparent they hadn't come to pay their respects; they had come to celebrate his death.

Phillip Longtree was the final interview and the most promising. During the hour-long session they determined that Phillip had met Roy in detention as a juvenile and had been friends for the past 15 years.

Phillip also had an extensive criminal record, primarily for offences against women, consisting of three charges of domestic violence against two partners and an attempted rape of a 12-year-old girl when he was 14.

After the interview Phillip was allowed to leave and they summarised the afternoon's work. They agreed that the best lead from the day's investigations was Phillip and hoped they would get more information when they interviewed the family the following morning.

Roy's death was considered suspicious but hadn't been declared a homicide. Peter's phone beeped; it was a system-generated message from the DNA Crimes Database. The system had identified a match in DNA to Homicide Case BI12675X.

Peter said, "Come on, Kim. We have a lead." They walked to Peter's office to log onto the system.

The DNA match was for a ten-year-old cold case; a home invasion, five perpetrators, a mother murdered, and the daughter critically injured. They sat silently for the next 25 minutes as they read the police report, medical examiner report and hospital reports on the mother and girl. Peter looked at Kim whose face was white. He was close to discharging his stomach contents.

"Jesus! Those poor women. Those men were monsters. How could they still live in society after committing such atrocities?"

The investigator of the case was Senior Detective Shane Edwards. Peter looked him up on the system. He was still on the force and had a contact number so Peter called him. It was 8:00pm. Shane Edwards answered the phone on the 4th ring. "Hello?"

Peter introduced himself and said, "I am investigating a homicide and have a DNA match with a home invasion for which you were the lead investigator. Aiko Bianchi was murdered and her daughter Sakura Bianchi was critically injured. Do you remember it?"

There was a pause. Peter thought he heard a faint sob and then Shane spoke softly, "Yes, I remember; it has haunted me ever since. We could never provide justice for the little girl or her mother."

Peter said, "We would like to discuss your investigation to determine if there are any factors to help solve another case."

Shane said, "Come to my office at 7:00am tomorrow and I will tell you what I know." Peter and Kim departed and went to their homes. It had been a long day and sleep didn't come easily to either of them as their thoughts kept returning to the police report they had read.

***

The next day, at the agreed time, Peter and Kim met in Shane Edward's office. After the mandatory greetings, Peter outlined Roy's death, reciting the medical examiner's assessment and confirming samples of Roy's DNA matched one of the home invaders from the cold case ten years ago.

Peter knew Shane was in his mid-fifties, however, the man sitting across from him looked to be in his sixties. His nose was bulbous with red veins covering most of its surface, obviously resulting from years of heavy drinking. The job must have weighed heavily on his health.

Shane began, "I got the call at 11:00pm, I was at home, and the chief wanted me on site asap. I quickly dressed and was there in 10 minutes. Two patrol officers stood outside the house flanking a man with a dog on a leash. An ambulance's flashing red and blue lights eerily illuminated the night's darkness. The other homes in the street remained in darkness, unoccupied; what appeared to be a well-populated area was actually quite remote.

I motioned to one of the officers to join me and after he had walked over, I said, "Brief me quickly."

He said, "It appears to be a home invasion. The man with the dog called 000. Inside are a woman and child; the woman is dead, and the child is near death. The paramedics arrived two minutes ago and are treating the girl."

"I left the officers with the witness and walked inside the house. It was a house of horrors. In all my years of investigating I had never seen a crime scene like this before. Blood was everywhere. The paramedics had placed the naked young girl on a stretcher. They had applied an oxygen mask and one paramedic was inserting a cannula in her arm to start a saline drip whilst the other applied bandages to the young girl's chest. She appeared to have been stabbed multiple times and was covered in her blood. A pink nightie decorated with a floral pattern lay beside the lounge chair. The mother lay on the bed in the bedroom with her head hanging over the edge. A savage cut to her throat had almost decapitated her. She was naked and I could see extensive bruising to her body and several bite marks. She was also covered in blood. The wall next to the bed had arterial spray to the ceiling. It looked like a scene from a horror movie.

I asked a paramedic about the girl's condition, and he said, "She is critical, has a faint pulse and has extensive blood loss from knife injuries. She may not survive."

"I looked around the small house. The paramedics had contaminated the crime scene when attending to the girl. I had worn my surgical booties over my shoe and hoped we could obtain solid forensic evidence from the bedroom. I needn't have worried though because the medical examiner had obtained multiple semen samples from the mother. The

70

nurses at the hospital used a rape kit to secure multiple semen sources from the young girl.

There were three masks scattered around the room. I went outside and found two additional masks. The witness's name was Michael Winton; he had been walking his dog before bed. He said he often walked down the footpath at the edge of the creek to this street which was mostly deserted at that hour so he didn't have to worry about dogs barking.

I asked him to describe what he saw."

He said, "I was about 30 metres from the house when I saw the five men running out. Two had something on their heads which they discarded when outside. They jumped into the car and drove off with a screech of rubber and no lights. I couldn't see the number plate or determine the car's colour, just that it was a dark colour. Judging by the vehicle's shape, I am confident it was a Commodore sedan. I was deeply concerned as I knew the woman and little girl lived here alone. I had met them previously and we had spoken several times while walking my dog during the day. I went up to the front door and saw two masks lying on the grassy lawn. It must have been these that I saw the men throw away. The men hadn't bothered to close the door so I looked in and saw the little girl lying across a chair. She was covered in blood. I didn't enter the house and rang 000 immediately."

"His story matched what we found in the house. He appeared severely traumatised, so I suggested he go home and rest. I immediately called head office requesting traffic control stop any Commodore sedans in the area but we didn't find the men. That night when I arrived home, I entered my 12-year-old daughter's room. She was asleep. I kissed her softly and made a personal vow to find these men."

Peter asked Shane to tell them about the investigative process.

Shane commenced, "We cross-checked the semen samples with all known sex offenders within 100 kms of the home and didn't get any matches. The media had a field day pressuring us to find the culprits. Nothing they could say could motivate me more than my desire to find these animals. I had nightmares of that house for years. I was worried that they would re-offend, but as time went by the trail got colder. No similar cases ever occurred. We couldn't find any evidence that would lead to a suspect. We had their DNA on the computer system but nothing showed up. We were hopeful that we would get a DNA match sometime in the future and have a suspect to interview and potentially find all of them. I guess now we have the name of one of the perpetrators but cannot interview him."

Peter asked Shane what had become of the girl.

Shane said, "The homicide was prime news for at least five weeks. The current affairs program 60-Minutes ran a 30-minute segment releasing their names and showing family photos and videos from social media accounts. It was truly heartbreaking. The public knew the hospital where Sakura Bianchi lay in an induced coma. We were concerned that these men might try to silence her if she recovered so we provided her with a new identity. We told the media that she had never awoken from the coma and that the hospital had shut down the life support system. Sakura did recover after three months and we interviewed her. She had no memories of that terrible evening so another dead end. Knowing she remembered nothing from that terrible night eased my guilt from being unable to apprehend the offenders. The investigative team was stood down a month later, and then six months later the file was marked as a cold case."

Peter and Kim thanked Shane for his time and headed off to interview Roy's family.

Part 4

Training at the Temple

Twenty One

Sakura had been training at the Temple for six years. The training was demanding. Her daily chore was to carry water to the kitchen storage vats. It was a 100-metre trek from the ancient courtyard well to the kitchen vat. When she started all those years ago she had two five-litre stone jugs suspended on a bamboo pole that she carried across her shoulders. At first she could only manage with the half-filled jugs; however, after two years, she could take the larger ten-litre jars reducing the number of trips to fill the vats.

Master Ming congratulated her when she had reached this level and explained that the combined weight of the two ten-litre stone Jugs and the bamboo pole was 25kg. Over the years, this weight training had strengthened her shoulders and legs. At that time Sakura only weighed 40kg so she carried more than half her weight over a kilometre daily.

After years of training she would leave the Temple weighing 48kg, primarily due to increased muscle mass. She had very little fat.

Master Ming provided her with two new jugs, shaped differently, with narrow mouths and no handles. He explained that these could hold 10 litres each and she was to use these jugs now to fill the kitchen vats. They were to be held by the neck with her fingers to strengthen her grip. Initially, she struggled, her grip too weak to carry the jugs when full. Instead, with the jars partially filled, she had to make 100 trips, a journey of 10 km.

At night her hands would ache, her fingers swollen from the effort. She needed to get up at 4:00am every morning to complete the chore before her morning training and start before breakfast. She endured these early starts for the first two years. By then, she could carry the jugs full.

By the end of two more years her hands had strengthened and she could complete the chore quickly. Her grip strength was incredible. In the past year no student had dislodged any weapon from her grip.

Morning training included weight training. Her favourite exercise was the suspended jars—two ceramic pots filled with granite stones suspended on a bamboo rod held across the shoulders. The combined weight, almost 80kg, was twice her weight. She would alternate between squats and walking lunges. She was the strongest student in the Temple for this exercise on a weight-to-power comparison.

This training had strengthened her glutes, quads and hamstrings so that she could leap her height from a stationary stance. She felt proud of her body now. The scars no longer concerned her. Her focus was to be the best she could be.

Once a year the Temple held a tournament called the Michika. Mirako had missed Sakura's 17th Birthday using her once-a-year visit to watch Sakura compete in the Michika. This event selected 64 students from the school separated into four groups. The groups consisted of students of all ages and both sexes. The winner of each group would compete in the final match where all four would fight until a victor was agreed upon.

The senior monks watched and judged each fight to determine the winner. Each group had 16 students and each student selected a bamboo rod from a decorative stone urn, 16 rods of eight different colours.

The day arrived and Sakura was surprised at breakfast to see Hirutu and Mirako eating at a breakfast table. It was the first time she had seen her grandfather since she had entered the Sohei Temple. She walked to their table and bowed to her grandfather then they hugged. Next, she turned to her grandmother and they hugged.

Mirako kissed her cheek and said, "I am so proud of you, Sakura. I am looking forward to watching you compete."

Sakura knew that to win the Michika she would need to defeat four students in her group and then win the final challenge. Master Ming was the judge of her group. Each student selected a rod from the jar. The end of Sakura's rod was blue and a young girl who had only been training at the Temple for six months held the other blue rod.

Master Ming had chosen the wooden tantō, a short sword of 30 cm, for the first round. Sakura quickly disarmed her opponent completing the event in 30 seconds without harming the inexperienced girl. Eight students remained.

The second round was to be fought unarmed and Sakura was up against an older student, a male who was 10kg heavier than her. She hadn't trained against this man before so she wasn't sure of his skill. He looked confident. He had a more extended reach and his weight would be an advantage if he pinned her on the ground.

He came at her, attacking with a roundhouse kick to her head which she avoided by ducking and countered with a sweeping leg which took his legs out from under him, slamming him heavily onto the ground. Before he could recover she punched his throat, halting the strike millimetres before contact. Ming announced Sakura as the winner.

Round three was against Niko who knew she was outmatched as they had often fought in training. Niko respectfully declined to compete forfeiting the win to Sakura.

Not having to fight meant Sakura could watch the remaining two boys' match; the winner would be her final opponent. Takahashi was the victor, a strong male who had trained at the Temple for 15 years. He was a formidable opponent and she had not trained against him previously. Wooden swords were the weapons for the final fight. Sakura felt confident as she had prepared for many years wielding wooden swords and authentic swords under Master Ming's tutoring.

They faced each other and Takahashi attacked with his sword raised above his head. He delivered a vicious downward stroke that would have shattered her shoulder if it had made contact. Sakura was no longer where he had aimed. She sidestepped to the left, dropped to the ground and rolled before jumping to her feet and taking a defensive stance.

He came at her again and stabbed the sword towards her belly. She pirouetted to the right, avoided his blade and struck down at his hand, the hard wooden sword crushing his fingers and forcing him to drop the sword. It was over. She had won. Now she would have the chance to win the Michika.

Temporary seating had been erected in the ancient courtyard allowing spectators to watch the final round. Sakura saw her grandparents seated in the front row surrounded by students' parents and guests who had also travelled to observe this tradition.

Master Shi Yan Ming addressed the remaining four students and said, "Today, you have demonstrated your skills to win your group challenge. You are the remaining four from 64 students and now we shall see who will take the honour of being the best in the Temple today. Fight with honour and respect remembering our primary principles."

Sakura studied her opponents, all male, all bigger than her and all senior students with several more years of training. They took their places and stood in a square formation four metres apart. The wooden staff was the weapon they would use, 2.5 metres in length, 30mm in diameter, an effective weapon that could strike from a distance.

Master Ming said, "Commence." The students bowed and assumed a defensive stance.

Immediately, the three males moved towards Sakura in a surrounding move. *Hmm*, she thought. So they had decided to eliminate her before battling against each other. She steadied her breathing and calmed her mind. She focussed on the sound of the footfalls from the opponent behind her whilst watching the two in front of her. With a yell, they came at her, all three at once, their staffs raised, a complex attack to defend against.

She raced forward and propelled her staff into the opponent's stomach on her left. He was entirely unprepared for this manoeuvre and expected her to defend. The vicious strike forced the air from his lungs and he tumbled to the ground, tangling the feet of the opponent on her right, and causing him to also fall to the ground. Sakura struck him with a blow to the side of the head—the fight was finished for both men.

Quickly she raised her staff above her head, her hands tightly gripping the staff shaft and preventing the blow aimed at her skull by the student behind her. The staff absorbed the force of the impact as she stepped back into her opponent, pushed onto her toes and torpedoed her skull into his jaw. She spun around to face him. Blood flowed generously from his mouth and her head throbbed from the strike but she was okay. His face had lost the confidence displayed at the beginning of the fight. They stood four metres apart. Both had taken a defensive stance, each waiting for the other to make the first move.

Sakura swung the staff with a sweeping figure-eight movement, first to the left, then to the right and slowly moved towards him, the tactic designed to intimidate. He decided to attack and moved forward quickly. With the staff held in front of him, his intent was to ram it into her stomach.

Sakura stepped forward and lowered herself, loading her powerful leg muscles for a leap. She pressed hard on her heels and launched her body into the air. The jump was incredible. She covered the three metres between them, avoiding his staff and attained a height of 1.8 metres - high enough for her to cheekily stomp on his head as she soared above him. She landed gracefully and sure-footed with her back to him and thrust her staff rearwards into his right kidney, a painful blow that ended the fight.

She had won! She turned to face Master Ming and bowed deeply. The crowd was silent, shocked by what they had witnessed, a fantastic spectacle performed by a petite woman. Three men were lying on the ground moaning, all trained and all bigger than her. She had defeated them in under a minute.

The sudden applause shattered the silence and birds took flight, startled by the noise, the crowd on their feet cheering. Sakura looked over at her grandparents both applauding enthusiastically. Mirako had tears streaming down her face. Hirutu stood with an enormous grin, his eyes glassy as he clapped furiously.

Sakura was overwhelmed by the ordeal. Her reward for winning today meant she would only be trained by the most skilled teachers, including

Master Ming, for her remaining time at the Temple.

Twenty Two

The sound of the courtyard bell woke Sakura. It was 5:00am, the start of the temple day. Today marked ten years at the Sohei Temple and it was her graduation day. Today she would become a Sohei Warrior.

Hirutu and Mirako arrived the night before and greeted her at breakfast. They told her how proud they were of her for achieving this level of competence, something very few students master, and to achieve this honour in just ten years was the first time in the history of the Temple.

The ceremony started in the afternoon with ceremonial fighting and Sakura demonstrated her skills to her grandparents and Master Ming. It was a fantastic display of grace, strength and ability. Afterwards, Shi Yan Ming summoned her to the dais where he was sitting. She bowed low before him, her ceremonial robes washing around her in the wind.

He asked her to kneel and then he presented her with a tsurugi sword. It was beautiful and over one thousand years old. The tsurugi sword was a slightly curved double-edged blade used in the 10th century by Samurai and Sohei warriors. It was an incredible honour for her to receive such a valuable gift.

Next, Ming presented her with her tantō, a short-blade sword to complement the tsurugi. It was another beautiful sword and was the blade typically used by warriors to commit seppuku. The final gift was a kaiken, a small dagger easily concealed within clothing.

He faced the assemblage of students. Everyone was present and he said, "Today, Sakura Bianchi, daughter of Aiko and Enzo, has become a Sohei warrior."

Sakura's soul pulsated within her, the sense of fulfilment and satisfaction impossible to describe as she fought to hold back her tears of joy.

That night the entire Temple feasted and celebrated her graduation. Every student with whom she had trained over the years congratulated her personally and presented her with a gift; something they had made. There were few material items here in the Sohei Temple, such as those available in the Western world.

The next day she left with her grandparents for Tokyo. She quickly settled back into her grandfather's home, savouring the exquisite luxuries compared to her years living in the Temple. She continued with her meditation and training each day performing katas and exercising.

On the fourth day her grandfather summoned her to the library. He had tea waiting for her when she arrived and some official-looking documents.

He said, "Sakura, I obtained these reports many years ago. They are the police and autopsy reports of you and your mother. As promised, these will provide more information about what occurred on that terrible night. Once you have read them we will plan justice for you and my daughter."

Sakura thanked him, drank her tea and commenced reading. The first folder was a police report. It was almost 5 cm thick, Aiko Bianchi stamped across the front. She opened the cover; the first section was the forensics report. Her mother had been found naked with significant bruising, her throat cut so savagely that she was almost decapitated. Sakura skipped forward to the medical report describing the physical damage to her mother and the semen samples detected in her body. Since they didn't know who the home intruders were, they just listed them as:

Assailant 1 - Semen sample found in victim's anus.

Assailant 2 - Semen sample found in victim's vagina.

Assailant 3 - Semen sample found in victim's vagina and anus.
Assailant 4 - Semen sample found in victim's stomach.
Assailant 5 - Semen sample found in the victim's vagina and stomach.

The last section of the report was the autopsy report. Sakura considered reading it, then decided against it. There were some things she didn't want to know.

Next, she opened her police report. It was also very thick and had Sakura Bianchi stamped across the front. The medical information described the physical damage to her body and the semen samples detected in her mouth, anus and vagina. In Sakura's report, they used the same approach to describe the home invaders.

Assailant 1 - Semen sample found in victim's anus.
Assailant 2 - Semen sample found in victim's vagina.
Assailant 3 - Semen sample found in victim's vagina and anus.
Assailant 4 - Semen sample found in victim's mouth and anus.
Assailant 5 - Semen sample found in victim's vagina and mouth.

She started to cry, she had suspected she had been sexually assaulted but this was a cruel, malicious attack on a young girl. She could never have imagined the extent of the atrocities inflicted upon her or mentally prepared herself to accept what happened. Her emotions cycled between despair and anger, an overwhelming sense of betrayal and a desire for revenge.

Her grandfather walked over to comfort her. He hugged her, "It's ok, Sakura. Let's spend some time planning our revenge to achieve justice for you and your mother."

It took a couple of weeks to develop the plan and a few more months to obtain passports and the supplies required to execute the mission. Then they were ready. Sakura was excited that after ten years of preparation she could finally put her skills to actual use.

Part 5

Present Day

Mr Duck loses his Quack

Twenty Three

Sunday 31st January

Sakura awoke in a pool of sweat. The nightmares had returned since she had read the police reports back in Japan. She could only remember parts of that terrible night. Tonight's nightmare played on her mind like a movie. It was surreal for her to see herself and her mother in such detail.

In her dream she was sitting next to her mother on the couch in their living room, watching TV. She remembered that they had recently returned from a holiday in Bali where they had enjoyed a wonderful time. She knew this because her hair was braided. The Balinese woman who had toiled over her hair for 60 minutes had tied a bead at the end of each braid. Sakura was watching TV smiling, running a braid through the palm of her hand. Her hand would stop when it reached the coloured bead at the end of the braid.

She remembered how she had enjoyed the feeling of the braid in her hand. She was dressed in her favourite nightie, her legs curled up under her, hidden by her nightie.

Suddenly, there were five men in the room, all wearing masks. Her mother instantly leapt into action and struck the first man hard in the

84

solar plexus and he bent over in pain. The others had not expected this and she was able to hit another with a blow to the nose that drew blood. When he reached up with his hands to his nose, she kicked him hard in the groin. He groaned dropping to his knees. The remaining three men grabbed her and she was quickly overpowered. Her mother looked so small against these men. It was a hopeless situation. Four of the men dragged her mother into her bedroom, each man holding an arm or a leg. Her mother was totally defenceless.

A man in a duck mask leered at Sakura and walked towards her, grabbing her arm so hard that it hurt. He then pulled Sakura's nightie over her head and forced her over the back of the lounge. He was so much stronger than her. She started to cry not understanding why this was happening to her. She heard men in her mother's room yelling, some laughing; they sounded like mad men. Then she screamed out in pain as the man in the duck mask forced himself into her anus.

Sakura looked across at her alarm clock. 4:00am was displayed in green numbers on its digital LCD face. She decided to get up. She swung her legs out from under the sheets, sat up, placed her feet in the slippers she kept under her bed and walked into the kitchen to prepare a pot of tea. Today she was completing the special surprise she had for Phillip.

The instrument had been machined in Japan and shipped to her in three separate packages during the first week she had been in Australia. The device required a small explosive charge to operate. It wasn't possible to send explosives in the post as they were easily detected, however, Sakura had been trained in the manufacture of explosives and had purchased the necessary household products to fabricate the explosive charge.

She took a sip of her tea then set to work. First, she placed a large pot on the stove and ignited the gas. She removed a container of dishwashing detergent gel from the cupboard under the sink along with a container of ammonia.

She emptied the contents of both containers into the pot and stirred it until it started to boil. Then she reduced the cooktop flame to low, allowing the mixture to simmer over the next two hours. Next she took the three packages out of the bedroom and emptied the contents onto the kitchen table.

The first package held a structure that would be the base. It was 150mm square and made from a solid 5mm thick piece of aluminium. Attached to the base was a cylinder with a diameter of 100mm and a height of 15mm. The explosive charge would be contained within this cylinder. The base had four threaded holes in each corner and these would be used to secure the second stage to the base once the charge had been included. The second package held the working components and the third package held the electronics and remaining parts for the device.

After two hours, Sakura checked the pot for the final time. The process of heating the chemicals had transformed them into a malleable solid, similar in consistency to plasticine. She had cooked up a powerful ammonium nitrate explosive. She pulled rubber gloves onto her hands, weighed 50 grams of her explosive and placed it in a mixing bowl with 20 grams of aluminium powder. She kneaded these together until the aluminium powder was consistently distributed throughout the plastic explosive.

She opened a container of diesel fuel, measured out a small amount and combined this with the explosive, kneading it evenly into the explosive. The diesoline increased the explosive force by a factor of ten and the aluminium powder increased the heat generated and the cylinder's internal pressure. She packed the charge into the cylinder, installed the electrics and tightened the bolts finalising the assembly.

The device was activated by a Bluetooth app on her phone using an encrypted key. She opened the detonation app on her phone. It was a simple interface with three lights in a vertical format like a traffic light. Next to each light was a digital button. At the top was a green light, the word 'Safe' in the button; below this was an amber light with the word 'Retract' and the third light was red with the word 'Boom'. She pushed the 'Safe' button and the green light illuminated confirming communication with the device and that it was in safe mode.

Tomorrow she would be visiting Mr Duck.

Twenty Four

Monday 1st February

Sakura had spent the past two weeks undertaking surveillance on Phillip Longtree, aka Mr Duck, who lived in Revesby and Barry Shrimpton, aka Goofy, who lived nearby in Bankstown. During that time she had gained access to Phillip's garage code using a device her grandfather had provided and she could enter or leave as she liked.

She had decided the garage was ideal for her next attack. It was a solid brick structure positioned below and in front of the main house. The garage roof was a concrete slab used as an outdoor patio with a table and two chairs on it. Access to the garage from the house was by two flights of stairs. This had two advantages: she could access the garage and it was unlikely anyone in the house would hear her; also, anyone going from the house to the garage was easily visible.

Like the first assassination, she needed to make Mr Duck's death appear to be an accident. She didn't want to scare off the remaining assailants before she had dealt with them.

On Monday at 2:00am she parked her Commodore three blocks from Phillip's rented property and walked along the deserted street. She opened the side door of the garage with her lock picks. 20 seconds was all it took for this cheap lock. Phillip's car was an old 2002 Commodore with fading paint and damage on most panels. It was a solidly built vehicle and perfect for her needs.

She squirted a generous volume of super glue into the driver's seat belt release button, which, once set, prevented its operation. The seatbelt could still be fitted into the locking buckle, however, could no longer be unlocked.

Next, she placed her device under the driver's seat positioning it directly below where Phillip would be seated. She was disgusted by the filth on the floor of his car - cigarette butts, food droppings and a used condom had found a home under the driver's seat. She had pushed these aside so her device was stable on its base. She locked the garage door and walked back to her car and drove home for a few hours of sleep.

Twenty Five

Sakura held her nose, took a deep breath, then sat at the bottom of the pool and counted to five. The water felt cool on her skin after the heat of the Balinese sun. Pushing hard against the pool's bottom, she surfaced like a killer whale chasing prey. She shook her head to the left, then right and left again. Her braids flew out from her head, water streaming off them and soaking her mother who was laughing and holding her arms out to protect herself.

Her eyes opened and she hit the alarm *Stop* button on her clock at 6:00am. She had recently started dreaming of her mother and herself together, a pleasant change from the nightmares which had permeated most of her nights over the past ten years.

She got out of bed and dressed. Today was Phillip's day. She hoped that after dealing with Phillip she would have fewer nightmares and more dreams of her Mum and Dad.

She rode her Ducati past Phillip's house and settled the big bike on its side stand at the park's end of his street. She walked casually to his house, glancing at her watch. It was 7:20am and he would be leaving for work soon. She looked around. The street was busy, people travelling to workplaces, mentally planning their day and paying little attention to her. She hid behind a Hibiscus tree near his garage, a place she had selected during her reconnaissance, providing cover from the street and house.

Twenty Six

Phillip got out of bed. It was Monday morning and he readied himself for work. At 7:30am he closed the house door and walked down the stairs to his garage. He entered by the side door and pushed the remote on his key fob to open the garage door.

He didn't see Sakura as she quickly rolled under the opening garage door and hid behind the Commodore. Phillip opened the driver's side door and sat down. He clicked his seat belt into place and as he inserted the ignition key, he felt an excruciating pain in his lower body.

When Sakura heard the seatbelt click into the lock she sent the *Close* code to the garage door to limit the noise that could be heard from outside.

Using the Bluetooth app on her phone, Sakura activated the device she had named Phillip's special surprise. Two AAA batteries sent an electrical charge into 50 grams of ammonium nitrate, igniting the explosive. Instantaneously the internal cylinder pressure increased from 32 to 3,000 psi, disintegrating the thin barrier between the base and the second stage, which housed a 5cm steel harpoon. The harpoon was propelled upwards at 800 metres per second. It easily penetrated the seat, then entered Phillip through his rectum and an attached wire trace halted its journey 30cm into his body.

The device was modelled on the technique used to harpoon whales; an activity still carried out by some Japanese fleets. The harpoon was now fixed securely inside his abdomen, immobilising Phillip to his seat. Sakura could hear him swearing, his body in shock, not yet registering the extent of his injury. She moved swiftly to the passenger side and entered the car.

Phillip's stunned body and confused brain were trying to understand what was happening when the small Asian girl opened the passenger door, sat and said, "Hello, Mr Duck. Do you remember me?"

He immediately knew who she was. When he last saw her, she was only a small girl, almost 11 years old. That was about ten years ago. He wondered if she was responsible for Roy's death. That was when the pain in his stomach started. It felt like molten lead and he began to scream when she quickly slapped tape across his mouth to quieten him.

"Hello Phillip, we will have a little fun, like the fun you had ten years ago. You remember when you sodomised me and my mother? I thought a fair punishment for you would be something similar."

Phillip shuddered in fear. He thought she was dead. Mark had stabbed her three times. The media had reported two fatalities from the home invasion.

Sakura continued, "Phillip, first I want you to answer a few questions and perhaps depending on how honestly you answer them, I will release you." She asked, "Were you wearing the duck mask?"

Phillip started to cry and nodded his head.

"Was Alex Webster the man who killed my mother?" He nodded.

"Was Mark Chisholm the man who stabbed me?" Again he nodded.

"Do you know where Mark and Alex are living now?" He shook his head.

Phillip was crying; his eyes were wide with fear and pain.

"Now, Phillip, I will remove the tape from your mouth so you can tell me how sorry you are. If you are convincing, I may call an ambulance for you."

She removed the tape from his mouth and waited for his apology. As he started to say he was sorry, she reached down into her left motorcycle boot and removed the kaiken from its sheath. With the speed of a cobra she grabbed his tongue and pulled it hard whilst striking down with the razor sharp blade. There was hardly any resistance.

Phillip was horrified. She was holding his tongue in front of him as though it was a valuable prize. He couldn't scream and made a gurgling sound as he attempted to unbuckle the seat belt but it wouldn't undo. Frozen by pain and fear he could feel the fluids gathering on the seat under him. Looking down he saw himself sitting in a puddle of blood, urine and poop.

He looked across at her and she was smiling. He could see she was enjoying this.

She had her phone out now and said, "Phillip, let me help you remove that nasty arrow shaft."

Sakura tapped a button on her phone app, which instructed the device to commence its second function: to retrieve the arrow, much like a harpoon gun. The wire trace on the tail of the harpoon was connected to a small winch. The drive transmission from a toy remote-controlled car powered the winch. When activated, the motor started to rotate the winch winding the wire trace onto it. The whaling ships used larger engines on the harpoon guns; of course, they could pull in a 150-tonne blue whale.

Slowly the harpoon was being pulled from Phillip's body. Unfortunately for Phillip, the barbs on the point of the harpoon were embedded into the surrounding flesh. Poor Phillip's body would offer little resistance against the harpoon barbs as they retracted along the same route they had entered.

Sakura knew this would be excruciatingly painful and Phillip was frantically moving as much as he could in his restraints. There was a muffled scream as the harpoon retraced its journey to depart his body, dragging flesh and leaving a gaping wound. With a wet-sounding whoosh, the miniature harpoon was pulled free and a massive lump of flesh containing parts of his bowel was attached to the barb.

Phillip looked at the woman as he began to slowly bleed to death. Although the harpoon no longer trapped him, the damage to his body prevented him from moving and he was still held in place by the seat belt.

He watched as the girl opened a jar, deposited his tongue into a clear fluid and sealed it. *'Mr Duck'* was written neatly in black ink across the label. He started to feel faint, the pool of liquid he was sitting in growing more extensive as it ran freely from his body. It began to drip from the seat onto the floor of his Commodore and was puddling in the foot well near the vehicle's controls.

Sakura exited the car, opened her backpack and removed a Phillips head screwdriver. She climbed under the car, found where the fuel filter joined the main fuel line to the petrol tank and loosened one end until she had a steady fuel flow.

Next, she opened the valve on the LP gas bottle attached to the Weber barbecue. Then she opened the 10-litre fuel container Philip used for mowing, emptied the liquid over his lap throughout the car and poured a trail to the barbecue. She opened the driver's side rear door, removed her harpoon device and stored it in her backpack after cleaning it and discarding Philip's body parts.

Phillip was almost unconscious when she came to the driver's side door. She held up his head which had been resting on his chest and smiling, she said, "Goodbye Mr Duck, I hope you had fun." She started the car and the fuel line generously spurted the flammable petrol onto the garage floor.

Sakura lit her incense pyramid and placed it at the rear of the garage, judging that it would take at least 5 mins before the fuel leaking from the fuel line reached it. She exited the garage and walked towards the park where she had left her Ducati Monster.

She waited a few minutes watching the house when suddenly, the quiet street was jolted by multiple explosions. The concrete roof was torn from the garage and settled four metres away on the neighbour's lawn, as flames leapt from the garage rising 20 metres into the air.

Sakura smiled, said, "Quack! Quack!" then turned the key in the ignition and hit the starter button. The Ducati roared to life and she rode home.

Twenty Seven

Detective Peter Reynolds answered the ringing phone; it was the chief. "Reynolds, we have another suspicious fire and death. The address is 22 Bond St, Revesby and the occupant is Phillip Longtree. The computer flagged him as a potential suspect in your investigation of Roy Homer so I'm assigning this case to you."

Peter wrote down the details on his notepad and looked at his watch, 9:30am Monday morning; not a great way to start the week. He had made zero progress on the Roy Homer case from two weeks ago. Perhaps this was related and they could get a lead.

He said, "Kim, let's go, I'll brief you in the car." They drove to the address; the fire brigade was packing up and the forensics team was on-site. Peter looked around to survey the scene.

The garage had exploded, most of the blast had been directed up and out. The only remaining wall was at the rear. It had withstood the blast due to it backing onto the hillside behind it. There was a massive slab of concrete in the yard next to the house which had obviously been the garage roof. What looked like a garage roller door was lying in the front yard of the house directly opposite.

The front and side walls had disintegrated and the bricks were strewn all over the street. Most of the windows of the houses on the opposite side of the street had been smashed by flying debris. A burnt-out car shell was leaning over in the flooded garage, part of it lying up against the rear wall. The car doors had been blown open and were facing forward in a position for which they were never designed. The car roof had been torn apart as though a missile had exploded from within.

Peter and Kim walked up to the site and Peter asked the lead forensics officer for a report. The officer's name was Ken Roberts and he said, "Initial observations indicate two ignition sources. The car's petrol tank has exploded and this has been the primary source of the vehicle damage. A 9kg LP gas bottle has also exploded probably due to the initial fire source and this combined with the car explosion has destroyed the building. In the yard across the road we found two body parts, a jawbone and part of a foot. These were superficially burnt so we should be able to retrieve DNA samples from them to help identify the owner. I'm assuming the deceased had started the vehicle which was the ignition source for the explosion. We will take the vehicle back to the yard and run tests against it to determine why it exploded. It's going to take time though to piece it all together; parts are being found within a two-block radius."

Peter was wondering if these two deaths were related, a possibility if the body was confirmed as Phillip Longtree. Both these men were friends and both had extensive criminal records. Peter asked Ken to get the other uniforms to start door knocking to interview the neighbours to see if anyone had seen anything. They only had to wait 5 minutes and the medical examiner arrived. The three of them walked past the debris. It looked like a war zone as they entered the garage.

Inside the car was a partial body, the legs were gone as were the arms and head. It appeared that the body trunk had been restrained in the seat by the seat belt initially before it had melted away. The chest had been cleaved open from the blast and the entire body was charred so badly that the medical examiner said it would be difficult to obtain DNA samples or confirm whether the cause of death was accidental or homicide. He asked Peter to get more uniforms there and do a sweep of the area for body parts to be delivered to his morgue. He would do the autopsy that evening and Peter could meet him in his office the following day for a debrief.

Twenty Eight

Sonia was daydreaming in Miss Anderson's math class. She was awakened when the bell rang, signalling the next lesson was to commence. She got up, walked towards Jodie, hugged her and said, "Enjoy your music class. I'm having an early lunch. I have a free session now, no subjects, yay!" She smiled, tilted her head and kissed Jodie on the cheek.

Both girls were in Year 11 and their birthdays were two days apart. They would turn sixteen in October this year. They had been close friends for the past four years, ever since they started high school and they did everything together. Unfortunately, Sonia could not join Jodie in music class due to her lack of ability. She had tried unsuccessfully to play the flute. Once, whilst practising at home, her brother had said cruelly, "Why don't you give it to Max to try, he would probably play better than you." Max was the family's pet Labrador. In that moment, Sonia decided she would no longer pursue music as a hobby or career.

Sonia ate lunch with Jodie every day except Mondays. Her mother could only afford to give her $40 pocket money monthly. That was barely enough to pay for her mobile data plan, leaving no money for other items like a nice lunch. Her parents didn't have spare cash for her despite both working. Jodie's parents, however, gave her $20 pocket money every Sunday night which Jodie used to treat herself to a hamburger for Monday's lunch.

Innocent Assassin

Sonia had prepared Vegemite sandwiches for lunch before she left home this morning. She walked to the school oval, sat in the grandstand and ate her lunch silently. It was a beautiful day. She was alone except for the twelve apostle birds fossicking insects in the grass, chatting with each other. They reminded her of when she had attended a Country Women's Association lunch with her mother. The birds behaved just like the older women there. They were funny and watching them made her feel happier.

Twenty Nine

Jodie packed away her flute and was satisfied with her performance in practice today. She thought all the students had played their various instruments well and managed to nail the composition as a group. Fortunately, it was finally coming together as the concert was in four weeks. She wanted to impress her parents on that night. She had been practising six hours a week over the past month in preparation for concert night.

The lunch bell sounded. Today was Monday and with $20 in her pocket, she planned to buy her favourite hamburger at the cafe just 500 metres from the school. It had become a weekly ritual. She loved these hamburgers.

As she entered the shop, an older guy was leaving. He was carrying a burger and blueberry soda, her favourite drink. Unfortunately, the soda cost $6, and $14 for the burger meant she would have no money left for the week, so she would just buy a burger. She craved for the soda now, having seen one so close.

She paid for her burger and when she left the shop, the guy was outside, standing by a car, holding the blueberry soda in his hand. "Hi, my name's Barry. I saw the way you looked at my drink in the shop. You looked sad. You can have it if you want."

"Why would you give me your drink?"

"You remind me of my niece; I feel like doing a good deed today. Pay it forward, so to speak. People who do good deeds usually have good deeds done to them in return. It's Karma."

Jodie considered it. Her mother had often warned her not to accept gifts from strangers. She did desire the soda though. She shrugged her shoulders, "Sure, why not! Thank you, that's very kind of you." She accepted the drink.

The man got into his car and Jodie walked towards the nearby reserve to eat her lunch. She sat on the wooden bench under the Melaleuca tree that provided shelter from the hot sun, removed the paper cover from the straw and, using the pointed tip, pushed the straw through the cling wrap into the soda and took a long swig. "Ahhh… that's so good," she whispered, then took another long drink before opening her burger and taking a bite. It was delicious!

Thirty

Barry had been watching the cafe for weeks, noticing that an attractive schoolgirl went there every Monday at noon. He had developed a plan which he would execute today. Earlier in the morning, he had purchased a blueberry soda from the cafe and when he returned home, he crushed two Rohypnol tablets into powder and poured the drug into the drink. Rohypnol turned clear liquids blue (this was to prevent it from being used for date rape), but the blueberry soda colour remained unchanged. He stirred the drink, then resealed it with clear wrap; it looked exactly as it had when he purchased it. He stored the Rohypnol soda in his car in a small ice filled esky.

He drove to the cafe, arrived at 11:40am and waited; the timing had to be precise for his plan to work. He heard the nearby school bell chime announcing lunch, waited five minutes and then went into the cafe to order a hamburger and another blueberry soda. He turned to leave the shop, pausing just long enough for the girl he was targeting to enter. He walked towards her holding his drink slightly higher than necessary to ensure she would see it. She had, and he could see from her stare that he had selected the ideal bait for his trap. When he returned to his car, he quickly switched the newly purchased soda with the one he had prepared at home and waited till the schoolgirl came out. She had fallen for his trap and accepted the doctored soda.

Barry sat in his car, leering as he watched the schoolgirl walk the short distance to the reserve, sit on the bench and start drinking the drugged soda. His heart was beating fast, his breathing restricted by anticipation, just harsh, quick breaths. The next fifteen minutes were critical for him to be successful. He watched the second hand of his watch slowly march its 360-degree path around its face. He could hear the tick, tick as the seconds passed, his senses amplified. Ten minutes passed. He started the car and drove the short distance to the reserve parking as close as he dared to where the girl was sitting. He waited five minutes watching her, his gaze as intent as a leopard stalking a helpless antelope for the family meal.

He saw her nod, followed by a pause, then she sat upright again. Time to strike! He quickly walked to the girl. He could see she was very close to losing consciousness. Placing his arm around her, he easily lifted her to her feet and walked her to the car, primarily supporting her as she slowly started to lose consciousness. She was utterly oblivious to what was happening to her. Holding her with one arm, he opened the car door, got her seated, and entered the driver's side door. He secured the seatbelt around her and latched it, ensuring she remained upright for their short journey. He was so excited he started to hum a tune.

When he arrived home, he drove into his garage, hit the *Close* button on the remote, shut down the car and took a deep breath. It had worked. He was in the safety of his garage and had direct access to his home from here. He looked across at the young girl studying her face. She was beautiful, her skin flawless except for two small pimples on her left cheek. He lifted her out of the car and carried her into his bedroom which he had prepared as a studio with five still cameras and three video cameras ready to record the next few hours of his pleasure.

***

It was 2:30pm and Barry felt very contented and sexually satiated.

606 Stop 203'. Using her school bus pass to pay, she walked to the second row and sat down. The bus was nearly empty which made her feel exposed, bare and barren. She sat silently, trying not to vomit again, until she arrived at the bus stop near her home.

Her mother wouldn't be home from work for several hours, allowing her time to clean herself up. She threw her underwear and school uniform into the dirty washing basket and ran a bath. Stepping into the tub, she was concerned the bath water would be too hot. Too bad, she thought, I need to soak. I need to get his stench off me and out of me. She lay in the scalding hot water, crying. When the water cooled, she pulled the plug and filled the bath again. She still didn't feel clean.

After sitting in the bath for 90 minutes, she dried herself and went to her room. She dressed in her nightie and lay down trying to feel innocent again. Until today, Jodie had been a virgin. She had not expected to lose her virginity in such a horrid experience.

Her mother entered her room when she arrived home from work to check why Jodie was in bed. Jodie told her she wasn't feeling well and needed to rest.

Jodie couldn't believe she had been so stupid. How could she allow herself to get into such a dire situation? Tears were running down her cheeks, her eyes bloodshot from hours of crying. She continued to berate herself; why had she accepted that drink?

There would be no solace in the privacy of her bed tonight and very little sleep.

Thirty One

It only took 20 minutes for Sakura to arrive home after saying goodbye to Mr Duck. Two of the five men were terminated. The years of training had been worth it. She was elated. Endorphins and adrenaline flooded her body, providing a euphoric wave of happiness. The combination of her second assassination and the rush from riding the big Ducati was overstimulating her.

She brewed green tea in her favourite teapot and turned on her MacBook. She removed the USB from its secret hiding space under the table and inserted it into the computer. She loaded the Ango-Ka app and saw that her grandfather had sent her a message. It simply said *the sample matches assailant 3*.

She typed, *Mr Duck's sample is on its way*.

She removed Mr Duck's tongue from the jar, sliced a thin section from it, put the specimen into a small plastic Ziplock bag, sealed it and placed it into one of the thick liquid-proof pre-addressed, postage-paid envelopes her grandfather had supplied, then returned the tongue to the jar.

She opened her mother's police report and located the section that detailed the DNA analysis. Then, using her brush and ink, she put a neat stroke through the words Assailant 3 and wrote Roy Homer. Just above where it described the body orifices containing Roy's semen, she wrote: *The not so bad wolf anymore*. She repeated this action in her police report, marking it similarly. Assailant 3 was the now-deceased Roy Homer.

104

Innocent Assassin

***

Sakura rode her Ducati to the post office to mail the DNA sample to Japan. Next stop was her tattooist for her second tattoo and another small ribbon straddled the scar that ran from the base of her neck to her belly button. Now she had two pink ribbon tattoos. She liked the way they looked. It made her feel powerful and confident. Only she knew their meaning.

She rode to the Four Seasons Hotel near Circular Quay in Sydney. At 1:05pm, she walked into the ground-floor cafe. A Japanese woman sat drinking coffee, a yellow plastic document folder on the tabletop. Sakura was carrying an identical-looking folder. She walked past the table, swapped the folders, and left the hotel without stopping.

She decided to ride by Barry's place, aka Goofy, to check on him and ensure he was there alone. She was planning on visiting him in the morning. She parked the Ducati a block away and walked towards his house using the opposite side of the street. The front door opened as she neared his home, and a young girl in a school uniform ran down the stairs. The girl was crying and ran towards the bus stop at the corner of the street.

So Goofy, it looks as though you are up to your old tricks.

Disgusted and appalled by the appearance of the distressed schoolgirl, she decided tomorrow would be Barry's final day.

She returned home and prepared Barry's specimen jar, neatly writing 'Goofy' across the label and filled the container with dimethyl hydantoin.

Thirty Two

Tuesday 2nd February

Peter was sitting at his kitchen bench finishing his breakfast of bacon and eggs on sourdough toast. He was planning the activities for the day. It was 7:30am. Almost 24 hours had elapsed since the second murder. He had been a senior detective for five years and knew time was the enemy. If motives and suspects weren't identified early, it became more challenging to solve a case.

He finished his coffee and drove his 10 year old daughter, Louise, to school. As she jumped out of the passenger seat, he said, "Louie, where's my goodbye kiss?" She wrinkled her nose and said, "Oooh, Dad, not in front of the school. That's gross. See you tonight." Then she blew him a kiss.

He watched her walk away and couldn't help thinking about Sakura. The home invasion from the past was intricately linked to his case and it was playing on his mind. He needed to find a connection. He wasn't sure how all the pieces fit together yet, but hoped he would unravel the mystery in time.

Kim had spent most of the evening assembling the evidence room with what they knew from Roy's homicide. He had included Shane Edward's information from the initial investigation. He had slept in the office, using the station shower in the morning and dressed in a clean uniform he kept in his locker for these occasions.

He met Peter in front of the medical examiner's office and they entered the office together. Tom stood at the mortuary table with charred body parts spread across it. They had collected approximately 60% of the body from the homicide scene. Some items had been ejected from the garage and were undamaged having avoided the inferno's ferocity.

Peter said, "We should be able to get DNA samples from some of these, Tom."

Tom nodded and said, "Yes, I sent samples to the DNA Crimes database last night for analysis. I marked it urgent and received the results 30 minutes ago."

He didn't say anything further. Eventually, Peter said, "And?"

"And the DNA matches semen samples taken from the mother and daughter in the home invasion case from ten years ago."

At last, thought Peter, *we are starting to get a view.*

"Can you summarise your autopsy results, please, Tom?"

"There was extensive fire damage from fuel and propane accelerants. The pressure would have built up quickly within the enclosed garage, resulting in a massive explosion that severely damaged the body. I can't determine if some wounds were inflicted before the explosion, with one exception. The victim's head was blown clear of the garage, over the roof of the house directly across the road and landed in the backyard. The head's journey resulted in additional injuries; however, the injury to the tongue is of interest. Or rather, the lack of a tongue."

Peter and Kim looked at him with puzzled looks. "Go on!"

"I found residual blood within the throat and mouth, indicating the tongue had been severed before the explosion and death. In my opinion, this is another homicide."

Tom continued, "Usually, I would suggest we engage the services of a profiler; it could be a serial killer. However, since both these men were involved in that home invasion, I suspect this is the work of someone seeking revenge, maybe a family member or a paid assassin."

Peter asked, "Any other information we can use to investigate?"

Tom said, "I assume this victim was also tortured, perhaps for information; maybe the perpetrator doesn't have all the names yet."

"Any leads?" Peter asked.

"Very little evidence is available to locate the killer. The fire destroyed all DNA from the crime scene."

Tom said, "These murders are well planned and executed meticulously. The person doing this understands police forensics and is well-trained. Maybe ex-military. Roy was a big man, so overpowering him would not have been easy."

Peter and Kim nodded their heads, thanked Tom for his conclusions and went to the cafe next door for a coffee and to discuss what they needed to do next. Peter called Ken Roberts, the forensics officer who led the team that interviewed the neighbours and asked him to meet them in the evidence room at 10:00am.

***

Ken Roberts was waiting for them when they arrived. He had used the morning to update the evidence boards to include details of the neighbours' interviews. Written and underlined on the whiteboard was: -

Abigail Hawkins - Interview 11:00am

Peter said, "What can you tell us?"

"Yesterday was a long day. My team didn't finish interviewing the neighbours until 9:00pm. The neighbours were shocked by the mess, destruction, and death of their neighbour. I doubt any of them are suspects."

He continued, "To summarise, the deceased had kept mostly to himself. No one knew what he did for a living. They rarely saw him outside and most contact was just a wave or a hello. They consistently said that he was quiet and he never had visitors. When I asked if they had seen any cars or suspicious people hanging around over the past weeks, there wasn't any useful information except for..." and then he paused for effect…

Peter said, "Abigail Hawkins."

Ken smiled and said, "Give the detective a cupid doll! Yes, she was fascinating, and if I were being polite, I would suggest she was the local neighbourhood watch. If I'm honest, I consider her the veritable nosy parker! She is in her sixties and spoke for at least sixty minutes. I didn't think I would ever get out of there. When I asked if she could come down to the station today to lodge a formal statement, well, you would have thought I was offering her the Australian Medal of Honour. She absolutely beamed and asked if 11:00am would be okay. She should be here shortly."

Abigail arrived a respectable five minutes early. Peter felt that she must have been near the precinct waiting for 11:00am so as not to arrive too early.

Abigail looked younger than her age and obviously took pride in her appearance. She was wearing a Burberry overcoat which she removed and hung over the back of her chair. Underneath the coat was a discreet aqua-blue mid-length dress, freshly ironed. They offered her tea which she accepted, asking for two sugars and milk.

Peter asked, "Have you seen anyone in the neighbourhood recently acting suspiciously?"

Abigail spoke voluminously for the next 60 minutes, describing four people she had observed over the past few weeks.

One man she suspected was having an affair with a married woman in number 54.

Another woman she had seen frequently walking up to the porches of houses, she suspected, was looking for home delivery parcels to steal.

The third person was a man with long, scraggly hair and the face of a heavy drug addict. She had seen him testing doors and windows at neighbours' homes. She was sure he was trying to steal from the houses but was too stoned to break in. She smiled when she said stoned, satisfied she had used a trendy definition, especially for her generation.

The fourth person was more attractive to the police. She said, "Last week, I saw a petite woman with Asian features walking down our street on the footpath opposite my house. She was wearing dark clothing, a motorcycle jacket and boots. Maybe she had just moved into the area as I'm sure I hadn't seen her before. She walked calmly and unhurriedly which surprised me. She had an athletic physique. I would have expected her to walk more briskly.

"She seemed to be interested in Phillip Longtree's house. She stopped in front of it, stared for maybe 30 seconds and then continued walking in the direction she was travelling. I also saw her the day before the explosion, walking on my side of the road and I got a better look at her. She's Asian, either Japanese or South Korean, I think. She has black hair and brown eyes and is quite attractive. She stopped and looked across the road at Phillip's house. She stood there for a minute or so watching, then turned and continued walking past my house. I saw her face, cold and expressionless, her eyes sparkling like black diamonds. I felt a moment of fear and danger. Then I saw her again yesterday after the explosion. I heard a motorcycle start up in the park at the end of the street. I was outside my house looking at Phillip's house with so much fire and smoke. I recognised her as she mounted the bike, then she rode past slowly looking at the house on fire."

Peter looked at Kim with a knowing look, their first real break. Perhaps this Asian woman was involved in the killings. Peter asked, "Can you describe the motorcycle?"

"It looked European, fancy looking, loud pipes, sounded powerful for such a petite woman and it was red. It had Ducati written on the tank."

They terminated the interview, turned off the recorder and thanked Abigail for her time. Peter asked, "Would it be okay to contact you if we have any more questions?"

"Of course!" Abigail said, smiling.

Peter turned to Kim, "Have traffic management check all the footage from the traffic cameras in the surrounding area for an image of the motorcycle."

Thirty Three

It was Tuesday morning and Sakura would be leaving Sydney today. She packed her suitcase with her outfits, Mac Book, Ango-Ka USB and placed everything in the trunk of the Commodore. She would leave her beloved Ducati Monster in the garage. She had a final look around the house. She would never return here.

She was wearing the police uniform her grandfather had organised for her. Today, she would drive the HSV Commodore which could easily pass for an unmarked police car.

Recalling the young girl's distress yesterday brought back memories of that dreadful night ten years ago. She remembered the sound of her mother crying in the next room. Sakura was in the lounge room, bent over the lounge chair; the man in the duck mask was sodomising her. Goofy stood before her; he was naked except for his mask. He grabbed her head, stuck his penis in her mouth, and said suck. When she refused, he thrust himself deep into her throat, choking her, vomit rising in her mouth. He pulled his penis out, let her breathe, and said, 'suck it, or I will do that again.'

Never had Sakura felt so helpless and defenceless; with the acrid taste of vomit lingering in her mouth, she sucked. What else could she do?

Sakura arrived at Barry's house at 8:20am, walked up the steps to the porch and knocked on the door. After a few minutes, Barry half opened the door, stuck his head out, looked at her and said, "What do you want?"

Sakura said in her sweetest, most feminine voice, "Hello, I am Constable Walters. There have been several burglaries in the area and I'm interviewing neighbours, requesting any useful information that could lead to arrests." She spoke composedly to give the impression that she had only recently become a police officer.

Barry thought, *good luck with me, darling, because I won't tell you anything to help.*

Sakura asked, "May I come in? I'll only take a few minutes of your time as there are only a few questions."

Barry had already drunk three beers this morning whilst watching the videos he took yesterday. He studied the constable. She was hot and petite and he liked them like that. He knew he could easily overpower this tiny woman. Barry couldn't believe his luck and thought these last two days were turning into the best couple of days ever.

He opened the door wide, stepped to the side and welcomed her into his home with a sweeping arm.

Sakura looked around. The house was a dump with overflowing ashtrays, empty cans and bottles of beer. *This guy is such a loser, the world will be a better place without him.*

Barry closed the door and studied her lovely swaying arse as she entered the room. Suddenly, she turned towards him and said, "You're looking a little goofy this morning."

What the fuck? "What did you just say?"

Sakura smiled. The words had worked and Barry looked surprised and *goofy.* She stepped towards him and struck hard at his right eyeball socket using her thumb and first finger of her right hand. The force of her blow crushed the fragile eye socket, allowing his eyeball to fall forward. She squeezed her thumb and forefinger around the eyeball and swiftly removed it from his head.

It was the first time she had done this to a man. The monks forbade this strike during training for obvious reasons, so she had practised with pig heads. She was surprised at how easy it was to remove the eyeball, much easier than on a pig. Her technique had been flawless. Barry's hands immediately went up to his empty eye socket, a predictable move.

Sakura steadied herself in her stance, then unleashed a powerful strike with her left fist between the 9th and 10th floating rib on the right side of Barry's body. The punch was delivered with incredible upward force, rupturing his liver.

The human liver is the largest internal organ in the human body. The force from the blow caused the liver to compress on one side and expand on the other, resulting in a pressure wave which over-stimulated the vagus nerve which runs along it. The Vagus nerve is the longest in the autonomic nervous system and is responsible for essential functions such as controlling breathing, heartbeat and blood vessel dilation. This disruption resulted in a widening of his blood vessels, except in his brain, and a decreasing heartbeat, which lowered his blood pressure. Barry's body went into an automated survival position, horizontal, in a last-ditch to save the brain. He collapsed to the floor like a rag doll.

Sakura carefully placed his eyeball in the jar, labelled in black ink with the word *Goofy*. She had practised the art of Shodo in the Sohei temple as part of her training and was delighted with her calligraphy ability. She undressed him whilst he was unconscious, then secured his legs together with his belt. During her interrogation training, she learned that subjects feel more vulnerable when naked and she wanted Barry to feel very vulnerable, just as she had felt when she was a little girl.

While waiting for him to regain consciousness, she explored his filthy house. She discovered the lights and cameras in the bedroom and knew immediately why the young girl was fleeing in tears. Goofy was a scumbag, no doubt about that. If Barry had been a little more attentive to her, instead of ogling her breasts, he would have noticed that she was wearing surgical gloves, disposable surgical booties over her shoes and a wig. Her previous two assignments required stealth and camouflaging techniques to provide her with time to complete her mission. Barry was her last assassination in Sydney, so a fire wasn't necessary this time. She didn't need to mask the scene; she planned to secure the site, leaving the house appearing undisturbed. She hoped he wouldn't be found for a couple of weeks as this would enable her to complete her mission in

Australia. He would be though, at some time, probably from the stench of his decaying body and then the videos and photos would be discovered. The world would learn about this depraved paedophile.

Sakura reached behind her and drew her tantō sword from its saya concealed inside her uniform. The tantō is a magnificent sword with a razor-sharp blade with cutting edges on both sides. When viewed from the end, the blade is a diamond shape. It is a very effective stabbing weapon.

Sakura positioned her blade between his shoulder and neck on his right side, then pushed the tantō blade under his collarbone into his brachial plexus. This group of vital nerves control the movements and sensations of the arm. The nerves are large, around 5mm in diameter, and branch and intermingle in a complex fashion. They begin at the spinal cord, pass between the vertebrae in the neck, run across the space from the neck to beneath the collar bone and through the arm.

Forcing the blade upwards, she severed all nerves before extracting the blade. She quickly drew her laser scalpel from her police belt, contained in the pouch that would generally hold the police pistol and sealed the wound to prevent bleeding. She repeated the process on the other arm.

Barry's arms were rendered useless. They would never function again but that was okay because this was Barry's last day anyway.

His breathing deepened and she decided it was time to wake him so they could have a meaningful discussion. She opened another pouch on her belt, removed the tube that contained the smelling salts and waved them under his nose.

Barry started to wake; he tasted blood in his mouth. He hurt badly!! The right side of his body was screaming at him. The police officer had struck him and broken something inside his body. She had also plucked out his eye like she was pulling a hair from his head. He wondered who the hell this bitch was.

Then he realised he couldn't move. His legs were secured, at least he could still feel them. His arms, though, were numb, no, not numb. It felt like they were missing. He turned his head, first to the right side, then to the left, visually confirming his arms were there, but still, he couldn't move them. She had done something to him and he realised he wasn't angry; he was terrified. His bladder let go and he could feel warm urine running down his thigh. He started to cry.

"Don't cry, Barry, you're a man and we need to talk. Do you remember me?" He looked up at her. She was attractive, with elfin features, petite, Asian appearance, nope, no idea who she was.

"No, I don't know who you are. Why are you doing this to me?"

"Well, Barry, let me help you remember. Cast your mind back ten years when you were wearing a silly-looking mask of a distorted face and you and your friends did horrible things to me and my mother."

Shit!!! He remembered that night; they were all high. Alex had told them about the house. The mother had died that night and the daughter a few weeks later. How could she be here now?

She smiled at him and said, "You were wearing that Goofy mask, weren't you, Barry?"

"Yes!" he said, nodding, his remaining eye shedding tears. "I'm sorry for what I did. Please forgive me, please don't hurt me anymore."

"I have some bad news for you." She turned on her laser scalpel and held it up for him to see.

"Barry, this is a wonderful instrument, it cuts like a blade and cauterises at the same time. That means no bleeding in case that word is unfamiliar to you. Let me show you how it works." Sakura reached down and, with a simple stroke, removed his left testicle and held it above his head so he could see it. She applied pressure to his mandibular nerve using her left hand, forcing his mouth to open. She dropped his testicle into his opened mouth, smiling as she saw how it filled the space. With one hand under his jaw to keep the mouth closed, she pinched his nostrils with the other.

"Swallow it! You told me to swallow. Let's see how you like it. Swallow it or die!"

Tears streamed from Barry's eye, and he swallowed.

"Very good. I think you should have another." Sakura continued his meal with his remaining testicle. Barry whined during the ordeal; he was pathetic. He was a poor excuse for a man. She wondered how many girls or women he had hurt or humiliated. Her anger grew inside her but she recognised it and calmed herself. It was negligent for her to become overly emotional as she knew that was when mistakes could occur.

Barry looked at her through his remaining eye. It was watery, and she considered taking it as a souvenir also, except she wanted him to see what was next. She returned her laser scalpel to its pouch, and from another, she removed a police baton and extended it to its entire length.

She removed her kaiken from another pouch on her police belt. The kaiken's razor-sharp 15cm blade makes it a perfect cutting instrument. She reached down, took hold of the head of his penis and cut it at the base of its shaft, removing the last of his genitalia. Blood started to drain from the wound. She held his penis above his head. He looked at her wide-eyed. "Now, Barry, we are going to have some fellatio."

She asserted pressure on his mandibular nerve again, his mouth opened, and she stuffed his penis into his mouth. Using the police baton, she pushed it deep into his throat. "How does that feel, Barry?"

He just gurgled some unintelligible words. Sakura sat patiently, watching Barry's restricted air flow choking him. He was slowly suffocating. After 10 minutes, he was still gurgling and she ended it by crushing his windpipe between her fingers. Countless journeys carrying water-laden jugs had developed her vice-like grip and she easily crushed his windpipe. Sakura watched the life slowly ebb from his body and Goofy was no more.

Sakura's face shone as she drove away, stopping to dispose of the wig, gloves, booties, police uniform and utility belt. She hoped it would be several weeks before Barry's body was found. Her next destination was Cairns where she would locate Mark Chisholm, aka Mr Mouse. She would miss Sydney and she would miss her Holden and her Ducati.

She stopped at the tattoo parlour for her 3rd ribbon; only two more remaining. The tattoos hid the evidence of her lifesaving surgery and the pink ribbons were helping to repair her emotional and psychological scarring. They illustrated her ability to heal and demonstrated how far she had come. They were a reminder of her strength. They would also be a reminder of this trip and what she had achieved.

She drove to the bank and parked in the rear car park. She removed the specimen jar from her backpack containing Barry's eyeball and prepared the DNA sample for Tokyo. She walked to the street and posted the DNA sample in the post box beside the bank. Then she walked into the bank to visit her safety deposit box.

***

Sakura parked the Commodore in the long-term car park at Mascot Airport and took the shuttle bus to the domestic airport. She expected to return to Japan before the airport realised the Commodore had been abandoned.

She was sipping on a chardonnay in the Business Class lounge, waiting to board her Cairns flight departing at 5:00pm. She used the remaining time to send a message to her grandfather using the Ango-Ka messaging app. It simply read, '*Goofy has eaten his last meal. I am leaving tonight for a holiday in Cairns.*'

There were no new messages from her grandfather.

Thirty Four

Peter looked at his watch. It showed 3:00pm Tuesday. He was anxiously waiting for traffic management to provide the information of the owner of the Ducati. He gave Kim a call. He picked up on the 2nd ring.

"Hello?"

"How are you progressing with the identification of that motor bike, Kim?"

"Come up to traffic management and I will brief you."

The Traffic Management Centre was two floors up and full of electronic equipment. It consisted of walls of monitors for real time monitoring, industrial air conditioning to remove the heat generated from all the equipment and four assessment rooms for checking photos and videos. Kim was standing at the front of one of the assessment rooms and said, "Come in and meet Tess."

Tess was a technician in her mid-twenties. Her hands flew over the controls as she watched the 12 monitors on the wall. "Tess, why don't you show Peter what we have." Tess pointed at Monitor 1 and said, "This was taken seven minutes after the explosion and is five blocks from the location, so it's a high probability this is the bike."

Peter could see an image of a Ducati motorcycle and a slightly built rider, probably a woman. He couldn't see her face as she was wearing a full face helmet with a black visor. He could see it was a Red Ducati

Monster. Unfortunately the motorcycle image was taken from the front so there was no number plate.

Tess pointed to Monitor 2, "This was taken a couple of minutes later, two blocks away." Peter could see it was the same bike.

He said, "We need a shot from the rear of the bike so we can get the number plate."

Tess said, "I've written a Python script which uses an Artificial Intelligence agent to search for me. It'll start from this camera position and check all the cameras within a 10 km radius. It uses pattern recognition to detect an image taken of the rear of the bike. I've constructed a rear view of the bike using the images from the traffic cameras and integrated these with photos from the factory for a 2020 Ducati Monster. It requires significant computing power and can only interrogate 2000 images a minute. I've programmed it to search for images which are time stamped 120 minutes before the explosion and 60 minutes after the explosion. There are over 300,000 images taken during this time period, so it could take up to 15 hours for a hit. I'd hope we'd get a result much sooner."

Peter understood most of what Tess said, even though he would admit that he had no idea what she had just done. He smiled at her and said, "That's excellent. Can you let me know when we have a hit and the name and address recorded for the registration of the bike?" Peter turned to Kim and said, "Get a Uniform to show these two photos to Abigail Hawkins. See if she can confirm if that's the bike and rider."

Thirty Five

Jodie got out of the bath, her third one today. She was finally starting to feel clean again. She dried herself, dressed in a fresh nightie and looked at her image in the mirror. Her face was puffy, her eyes bloodshot. She had dark circles under her eyes; she looked dreadful. It was 3:30 pm Tuesday. Her phone rang. It was Sonia.

"Hello?" She said softly.

"Hi babe, I missed you at school. Are you ok? It's not like you to have a day off?"

Jodie sobbed. She needed to share what had happened and Sonia was her best friend; she would understand. There wasn't anyone else she could tell, certainly not her mother. Over the next 30 minutes, she explained to Sonia what had transpired. Sonia was silent, just listening and waiting for Jodie to finish.

"Are you physically hurt?"

"Yes, a little."

"You need to go to hospital! You need to tell the police! We need this man punished for what he did to you!"

Jodie shouted, "No! I don't want people to know. I don't want them to look at me knowing what happened. I don't want the footage on the internet for everyone to see. I feel stupid, humiliated and violated."

There was a pause and then Sonia said, "He has probably done this before and will probably do it again to other girls. We can't prevent what may have happened to the girls before you but we can stop him from offending again."

"You can't tell anyone, Sonia! Promise me that you won't tell anyone! It will break my heart. I'm already struggling to deal with what happened. The thought of other people knowing will kill me."

"Ok, I'll keep silent, but I'm coming over to see you now."

"No! I want to be alone. I can't see you today, maybe Thursday."

Thirty Six

Sakura's flight landed in Cairns at 8:10pm. She had booked her ticket using her mother's name and credit card. It was a cheeky move, intended to leave a breadcrumb for the police to uncover in a few weeks.

Sakura and her grandfather expected the police to locate her before she had finished her mission, so they had developed a complex plan using a combination of fake passports, names, addresses, credit cards and an identity switch to throw the police off her trail.

On arrival in Cairns, Takeo, one of her grandfather's faithful guards, greeted her. Takeo had been in Cairns for two weeks. Her grandfather had sent him to find and follow Mark Chisholm. During that time, he had studied Mark's movements. Mark had worn the mouse mask and Sakura had confirmed with her previous victims that Mark had tried to kill her.

They drove to the hotel where Takeo had reserved two rooms. Sakura said goodnight, went to her room, had a hot shower and fell into a deep, peaceful sleep.

Thirty Seven

Peter was sitting at his kitchen table. It was Tuesday, 11:00pm and he was enjoying a glass of Merlot; it was his fourth. His wife, Janet, had just left the room for bed. He was considering the case, mulling over what he knew. He knew these two men had committed a terrible crime ten years ago so he had little sympathy for their deaths. He was more concerned about finding their killer. Someone was torturing and murdering these men, and there was a risk they might attack an innocent man.

Could it be this Asian woman? If so, how was she overpowering these much bigger men? Perhaps she is just the spotter and has an accomplice? The medical examiner had said it would require a massive blow to rupture Roy Homer's bladder. Would it be possible for this petite woman to generate the force necessary? Regardless, I need to find her. Justice is through the judicial system, not by vigilante actions.

He was also hoping to get a break in the Aiko Bianchi case. That family needed justice. The irony was that he didn't even know where Sakura Bianchi lived or her new identity. Her file was classified and required Supreme Court approval for access.

His phone rang. He answered. "Reynolds."

"Hello, Mr Reynolds, it's Tess from traffic management. I have a number plate for the Ducati Monster. It's registered to a Japanese tourist, Himari Miyagawa. Immigration confirmed she entered the country a month ago. I sent a squad car to drive by the residential address recorded on the registration papers. Unfortunately, she has recorded a false address. It was a derelict property."

Peter said, "That's great work, Tess, disappointing about the address. I'm not surprised. We're dealing with an ingenious killer. What do you have planned next?"

"I've submitted a computer batch job to search all the real estate rentals in Sydney, searching for leases taken out in the past 90 days under the name of Himari Miyagawa. I should have results in the morning."

"I'm glad you're on our side, Tess. I can't tell you the case details but I can say that it affects many people and if we can get a lead, we can save lives. Call me anytime when you get the results."

Thirty Eight

2 weeks earlier

Ichika was excited and a little anxious about what the next two weeks would hold for her. Several weeks ago, a friend approached her and asked if she wanted to make some extra money.

"How much?" she had asked. When they said 5 million yen, she asked, "Who do I have to kill?" and laughed nervously. She had agreed when told what she was required to do.

Now Ichika was sitting in the First Class Lounge at Narita Airport in Tokyo, drinking champagne, waiting to board her flight. She was travelling with a false passport as Nimiko Nakamura and was wearing the red ruby necklace they had provided. The passport photo showed a Japanese woman wearing the same necklace. The woman in the photo wasn't her; however, with a wig and some clever make-up, she resembled the woman in the passport photo.

The flight to Sydney, Australia, was uneventful and took less than 10 hours. Only two other people were in the First Class cabin; a couple in their 60s. First Class was terrific and she enjoyed the experience, knowing she would probably never fly First Class again.

She visited all the famous sightseeing places in Sydney and surrounding areas over the following two weeks. She had posted photos to the fake Nimiko Nakamura Facebook account and stayed at the high-end hotels. She had been provided with a credit card and had been encouraged to use it often for shopping, sightseeing, paying her hotel bills, and eating in the best restaurants. She was leaving an extensive digital trail.

Today was Monday, 1st February 2021, and she was sitting in the cafe of the Four Seasons Hotel. Before she left Japan, she was instructed to be at this location at this time and date. She had been given a yellow plastic document folder and told to insert the passport and credit card she had been using since entering Australia into the folder and leave it on her table.

She was enjoying a coffee when, at 1:05pm, a Japanese woman walked into the cafe. She was carrying an identical yellow folder. The woman walked to the table where Ichika was seated and exchanged the folders in a brief, fluid motion. It had happened so quickly that she only got a glimpse of the woman. She looked identical to Ichika; she was obviously the woman in the photo of the passport Ichika had used to enter Australia.

Ichika finished her coffee and went up to her hotel room. She opened the document folder which contained another passport, credit card, travel instructions and a first-class airline ticket to Singapore in the name of Himari Miyagawa. The passport photo was the same photo that was in the passport she had swapped. She would leave Australia today on Flight QF01 in less than 4 hours.

Ichika caught an Uber to Mascot airport. She was wearing the black wig and ruby necklace and had applied make-up to match the passport photo. The immigration officer looked at her passport and visa which indicated that she had arrived in Sydney on 4th January and stayed a month. He looked at her face, checked the photo and stamped the passport.

Sipping champagne in the First Class Lounge, Ichika reflected on the past 2 weeks. She had enjoyed her stay in Australia; it had been a paid holiday, and she wondered why? The woman with whom she had switched passports would now be travelling on the passport Ichika had used to enter Australia, and Ichika would be travelling on this passport. Why the switch?

Ichika decided the reason wasn't important. She hoped that she would be able to get home safely and that the Yakuza would deliver the 5 million yen she was promised and not kill her.

On arrival in Singapore, she checked into the Marina Bay Sands Hotel. It was late and she was tired. The hotel reservation was for five nights; however, the instructions left for her in the yellow document folder instructed her to leave the hotel on Tuesday at 6:00pm. She had awoken at 8:00am, showered, then gone downstairs and eaten breakfast.

As instructed, she spent the remainder of the day sightseeing and using the new credit card. She returned to her room at 4:00pm. She was to leave the hotel that night but make it appear that she was still staying there. She showered and then packed a small backpack with the new clothes and toiletries she had purchased that day, leaving behind her travel luggage, clothing, and toiletry bag.

At 6:00pm, she left the hotel and walked to the Marina. She found the boat referred to in her instructions and boarded. It took her to the channel where she boarded a magnificent yacht named 'Aiko'. She was shown to her cabin and, feeling relaxed, explored her quarters to find dresses in her size hanging in the wardrobe.

Six days later, Ichika arrived at Nagahamaura Bay. The trip was amazing. She had sunbathed on the deck during the day, and all the guests would dine together in a beautiful dining room, drinking expensive wines at night. The boat must have belonged to a wealthy, influential man, probably Yakuza.

Before docking in Japan, she was transferred to a smaller vessel and taken to an un-patrolled port. She was met by two men who drove her to a bus station and gave her a bus ticket to Tokyo. She handed them the passport and credit card she had used to travel to Singapore and they gave her a small bag. Inside were bundles of JPY10,000 notes. It was her payment; Ichika had never had so much money. She boarded the bus and wondered what she would do with her new wealth.

Thirty Nine

Wednesday 3rd February

Peter Reynolds was drinking coffee in his kitchen. It was 6:30am Wednesday morning. Two days had passed since Phillip Longtree's murder and he hadn't slept well. His phone rang. It was Tess from traffic management.

"Hi, Tess. Do you have any leads for me?"

"Apparently, Himari Miyagawa is a common Japanese name. I've identified six residential rental locations."

"Thanks, Tess. Please email the details to me. You sound tired?"

"I've been here all night; I'm going home to bed now. Hope the information helps."

"Thank you. I'll let you know how we go."

Peter rubbed his head. He could access two uniformed constables, Ken Richards and Beverley Hill. They would split into two groups: him, Kim, and the two constables. They could visit three houses each. It should only take a few hours. Excited, he rang Ken and explained they had six addresses. He said, "I have emailed you the list. You and Beverley take the last three addresses on the list. Call me if you find her or when you finish. Be careful. We're looking for a killer and we suspect the

129

woman has an accomplice, or perhaps even more people are involved."

Peter collected Kim and they drove to Arncliffe, the first address on the list. They knocked on the door and there was no answer. They decided to look around the side of the house and there was a window into the garage. Luck was on their side. They could see a Red Ducati Monster motorcycle parked inside. Peter's spine tingled with anticipation.

Was it possible the first address was where Himari Miyagawa lived?

He rang the chief and explained, "I need a search warrant to examine the house at Arncliffe."

"Ok, I'll have it for you shortly."

Next, he rang Ken, told him they thought this was the place and asked them to join him.

An hour later, he had the search warrant, two forensics technicians and Ken and Beverley to undertake a thorough search. They had moved the patrol cars away from the front of the house and closed the entrance door just in case Himari returned.

Peter's phone rang. It was Tess. He answered, "Tess, I thought you'd be asleep."

"I was sleeping until I got a system-generated message on my phone. Last night, I ran a job to search our transportation databases, buses, trains and planes for the name Himari Miyagawa. It took a while to consolidate the unstructured data from multiple providers."

Peter interjected, "Tess, that doesn't mean anything to me. I'll let you do the technology. Please tell me you have some useful information for my investigation?"

"Himari Miyagawa left Australia on Monday at 4:55pm flight QF01 destination Singapore."

"Thanks, Tess, you're the best."

He sighed. They had missed her by a couple of days. She must have killed Phillip and then gone to the airport to leave Australia.

Peter called the chief and explained what had happened. He asked if they could get ASIO to follow the international lead.

The chief said he would call in some favours and get back to him.

Three hours later, Peter's phone rang. It was the chief, "ASIO has confirmed that Himari Miyagawa arrived in Singapore on Monday at 10:15pm local time. She is staying at the Marina Bay Sands Hotel. Her booking is for five nights. She ate breakfast in the Hotel Dining Room Tuesday morning. She wasn't there when they sent two detectives to her room an hour ago. They have stationed a man in the foyer to watch for her. The hotel system doesn't record when the door is opened from the inside, so she could have left the room anytime in the past 24 hours. The system will alert them if her room key is used to access her room."

Peter had a queasy feeling in his stomach; had she eluded them again? It would be devastating for them to be this close and lose her.

Peter told Kim, "Let's leave the forensics guys to do the work here whilst we go back and update the evidence room."

Forty

Mark had left home at 5:30am to travel to his favourite fishing spot. He had been successful on many occasions fishing the incoming morning tide. Barramundi liked the early morning and fed upon the tidal flats. He was hoping to fill his esky with Barramundi fillets. The weather was perfect, 24C already, and the forecast was for 37C. He expected to be finished by 10:30am at the top of the king tide.

He walked to where he moored his 4.5-metre Quintrex, the 'Fishabout' model designed for estuary fishing. It was a nice Barramundi boat. He spotted a woman standing near the small jetty, her back to him. She was dressed in a black top and wore tight black slacks that accentuated her thin waist and full buttocks.

She heard him and turned towards him. She was petite, shapely, and had an elfin-like face with Asian features. He thought she couldn't have weighed more than 45kg.

What the fuck was she doing out here all alone so early in the morning? Silly girl.

He could feel himself getting hard. He thought how easy it would be to overpower her and start his day wetting his dick before he wet his line. Yes, today was turning out to be a wonderful day.

He stood before her, towering over her, at least 40 cm taller, and said, "Well, little girl, what are you doing out here all alone?"

"Same as you. I'm looking to do a little fishing. I just need to set my bait." She walked closer to him and suddenly, he couldn't breathe, an excruciating pain in his stomach. His vision faded to black.

Earlier, Sakura and Takeo had driven out to the place where Mark had his tin boat moored. They arrived early. Takeo had hidden the car from view and together they waited for Mark Chisholm. Takeo knew Mark enjoyed fishing on his day off and would come here to fish the incoming tide.

Sakura had seen the lustful look in Mark's eyes as they swept over her body. She thought, *Nothing has changed with you, Mr Mouse.* That's when she struck him with her powerful two-finger punch directly into his solar plexus.

The solar plexus or celiac plexus is a nerve bundle that, when hit with sufficient force, causes severe contraction of the diaphragm, resulting in complete exhalation of the lungs and a feeling of suffocation. Warning alerts go to other nearby organs, activating the sympathetic nervous system, resulting in sweating and a debilitating state of fear. Mark buckled over from the pain of his contracting diaphragm.

Sakura pushed through her heels, unleashing a powerful kick to his jaw. Mark's head snapped back, the force of the kick fracturing the intervertebral joints in his neck and damaging discs, ligaments, cervical muscles and nerves. Sakura knew the injury was painful and identical to severe whiplash from a high-speed motor vehicle accident.

Mark regained consciousness. He first noticed that he was lying naked on the tidal mud flats and couldn't move his hands or feet. The pain in his neck was unbearable. It felt like a knife was lodged in it. He slowly and painfully turned his head and saw his wrists bound with a cable tie to a star picket pounded into the mud.

The woman leaned over him and said, "Hello, Mr Mouse. Do you remember me?"

A feeling of dread overcame Mark.

Was this the little girl he had stabbed all those years ago? The news reports said she was critical, in a coma and not expected to recover. The media reported she had died three weeks after being admitted to the hospital.

They had done terrible things to the girl and her mother that night, the drug ice and booze driving their animal instincts. He had regretted his participation but not to the extent that he would hand his fellow home invaders to the police.

He said, "I'm sorry for what I did to you and your mother."

Sakura asked, "Mark, who killed my mother?"

"Alex killed her."

"Why did you try to kill me and why did my mother have to die?"

Mark started to cry and said, "You'd seen Roy's face; you may have been able to tell the police who we were. When Alex was raping your mother, she pulled down his mask and saw his face. We didn't want to kill you both. We planned to wear the masks so you couldn't identify us."

"You will pay for what you did to me that night. I have a slow, painful death planned for you. You are on the tidal flat and will become submerged by water over the next two hours, but first, I want to see if I can catch a couple of nice mud crabs. Mark, you are the bait."

Mark sucked in a deep breath, trying to avoid an anxiety attack. He had never been so scared! Unable to move, the tide would slowly flow over this mud flat and over him, as it had done daily for millennia. Already, he could feel soldier crabs nipping at his skin. This section of the river had millions of them, along with hundreds of mud crabs. The girl was holding a dagger above him.

"First though, Mark, I need a souvenir to remember you by."

He felt a pain in his groin. Looking up, he saw her holding his dick above him. She had removed his entire genitalia. He could see his scrotum attached to his penis, and he could feel the blood flowing from the wound between his legs.

He was in shock. She had taken his manhood! His heart was pounding, squirting his valuable blood from his body. The situation for him was dire for two reasons: firstly, lack of blood would kill him, and secondly, the scent of blood would attract predators. The water had already risen to his knees. The tidal mudflat sloped at about 30 degrees, so it would be less than an hour before the water was over his head.

Perhaps she is only trying to scare me.

Forty One

Once Sakura had disabled Mark, Takeo came out of his hiding place and carried him to the location they had selected for his final resting area. Takeo hammered in the stakes and Sakura applied the cable ties to his wrists and ankles. Takeo had purchased 20kg of chicken pieces and together, they scattered the chicken along the riverbank, a distance of 20 metres on either side of where Mark lay restrained upon the mud flat. Sakura was surprised at how quickly the groups of soldier crabs approached where Mark lay.

She woke him and enjoyed watching the fear in his eyes as she removed his dick and balls; he wouldn't need them again. She pulled out her special jar with *Mr Mouse* written on it and deposited her memento into the Dimethyl hydantoin.

"Mark, I need to prepare my bait, which is you, to attract the Mud Crabs. I hope you understand." She took out her kaiken and sliced off his left nipple. Mark screamed and so she removed his right nipple, another scream.

Sakura reflected on the months she had spent in hospital recovering from the injuries this man had inflicted upon her. She thought about the years spent training to enable her revenge. She was a warrior and he deserved this fate. Her grandfather and she had discussed for days how Mark should die. They had considered several scenarios, the criteria simple: it must be slow and painful, and he must feel completely helpless, just as Sakura felt on that horrible night. Takeo had participated in those discussions and, whilst observing Mark's routine over the past two weeks, had developed this plan.

He had prepared the required items before Sakura's arrival. Last night, he had explained today's program, and when he had finished, she kissed him. "Takeo, that's perfect. Thank you."

Sakura looked at Mark and decided his skin was too smooth, unlike her ugly red raised scars. She started to cut him, just small incisions, only 5 mm deep, angled like those a chef would make when preparing a piece of squid for cooking. She constructed a network of cuts which resembled a weave. Each cut bled a little, but not so much to be fatal. That wasn't her intent. Each incision was designed to attract…and attract it did. As the blood flowed into the river, the water now up to his waist, she could see the river was churning, boiling away from the banks, barramundi, mud crabs, sting rays and probably a bull shark or two. She smiled; today was going to be a day for Justice.

Mark's brain was confused; his body was in flight mode but couldn't go anywhere. He couldn't fight because of the restraints. More than a dozen soldier crabs were biting the flesh of his legs. It hurt like bee stings and he thought he could endure it until a powerful claw dug into the flesh where his pride and joy had been yesterday. It clamped down with incredible force and pulled a large piece of meat from his groin. A mud crab was eating him.

A fully grown Queensland mud crab claw has a gripping strength of 1500 newtons and can easily remove a finger. For comparison, the human bite can generate a force of up to 1,300 newtons at the molars.

Mark let out a scream.

Sakura squealed. "Takeo, I think we might have our first mud crab." Takeo grabbed the mud crab and deposited it in the 20-litre drum they had earlier half filled with river water. Sakura clapped her hands. "Oh good, we need a couple more." Mark's heart sank; he realised there would be no mercy and he was in deep trouble.

The river was lapping under Mark's chin. He had endured hundreds of soldier crab bites, and three mud crabs had dined on different areas of his body. He felt faint, drifting in and out of wakefulness as he slowly bled out. A swell washed over his face, into his mouth and receded. He coughed up the water, getting the girl's attention, and she came over. Mark pleaded with her, "Please, I don't want to die. I'm sorry. Please let me go and I promise I won't tell anyone about this."

He studied her. She was diminutive, yet her eyes betrayed her strength and hatred for him. He could see her impassiveness and thought, *I have never felt so terrified or helpless.*

Stone-faced Sakura said, "I will give you a chance. I endured ten years of hardship preparing for this day. I will let you live if you endure just three hours. In 90 minutes, it will be high tide and your face will be under 40 centimetres of water. Two hours later, the water will have receded. I will give you this snorkel to breathe. It's only 35 cm long, so you must lift your head to ensure it clears the high tide water."

Mark said, "The pain in my neck is excruciating; it feels broken. I don't think I can lift it for that duration."

Sakura smiled, "Well, in that case, Mark, you will die. You can either endure the pain or choose death."

She placed the snorkel in his mouth and returned to Takeo who had finished cooking the mud crabs. He had cracked them open and extracted the meat. He had prepared two generous crab rolls with lettuce in a thousand island dressing. Sakura scaled the bank and sat upon one of the folding chairs they had brought. She thanked Takeo for the crab roll and started to eat. It was delicious; it didn't get any fresher than that.

The snorkel Sakura had given Mark had an orange ring around the top, so it was easy to see when it was out of the water. It took another 30 minutes before the snorkel first went underwater and then she saw it reappear. She grinned; *I bet that hurt.*

She knew her kick was powerful, and the injury he had sustained was most likely life-threatening. It gave her great pleasure to know that his ordeal would continue for at least another couple of hours. She smiled each time the top of the snorkel cleared the water, knowing that each breath taken was accompanied by pain.

She remembered how difficult it was to breathe when she was in hospital recovering from her collapsed lung. People can't understand the fear of slowly suffocating unless they have experienced it. Mark was experiencing it now. He would know how it felt. He deserved to know.

The snorkel was above the water line now and she could see the orange ring; the tide had commenced its journey back to the ocean. Then she noticed the disturbed water, evidence of a tail hidden below, moving cautiously and deliberately following the blood trail. She recognised the unforgettable sign of a saltwater crocodile moving towards her captive. She saw the ridged brow over the eyes, just below the surface, belonging to a creature as old as the dinosaurs, possessing a simple reptilian brain that evolved for one purpose; to feed. It struck ferociously when it was within two metres of its prey. The water transformed into a boiling mass as the 5-metre beast gripped Mark's body and commenced its death roll. The crocodile's strength easily pulled the star pickets free from the mud. The cable ties fell loose as the creature rolled over and over, drowning Mark.

Then, slowly and silently, it retreated into the river.

Mr Mouse was no more.

Part 6

Ten Years Earlier

The Home Invasion

Forty Two

Aiko and Sakura had cleared immigration, collected their luggage and were waiting in the taxi queue. They had enjoyed a wonderful ten days in Bali and now they were tired and looking forward to returning home and relaxing. Aiko had three days' leave remaining before she needed to return to work.

Alex was sitting in his taxi. He was almost at the head of the queue after a wait of 90 minutes. He prayed for a reasonable fare when he saw the woman and girl. He put their luggage in the boot of his Toyota Camry and asked the woman where they were going.

Once underway, he asked, "Have you been on holiday?"

Simultaneously, they said, "Yes – Bali," and both giggled.

Alex asked, "What did you enjoy the most about Bali?"

The little girl squealed, "The monkeys were adorable, the sandy beaches white as the sun, the Balinese people were so nice." Then she said, "Look at my braids; it took 60 minutes and only cost $25. Aren't they beautiful?"

Alex smiled and said, "Yes, they are beautiful, and so are you and your mother."

Alex thought it strange when they arrived at their home as all the other houses looked empty. "Why are all these homes empty?"

The mum said, "A developer has purchased all the homes to construct high-rise apartments. Our neighbours and most of the street's occupants have sold as they were paid well above market for their properties."

"Why haven't you sold?"

Aiko sighed and said, "My husband Enzo and I built this home. I fell pregnant in this home and Sakura was born here. We have wonderful memories of Enzo. Now he is dead. We only have those memories. I fear if I sell our home, those memories will fade."

Alex said, "I understand. I wish you and your daughter a wonderful life." Aiko paid the fare, including a $10 tip.

Forty Three

It was a Friday night at the Bexley Hotel and as usual, Alex was there with his four friends watching the strippers. The group of five men had simple needs: booze, drugs and sex. Roy had scored the drug Ice, which they had all shared. It was the first time Alex had tried Ice and at first he was hesitant, but after 40 minutes, wow, man, what a rush. He was pumped and horny and reckoned he could fuck at least three women that night, a couple of times each. His sexual prowess was so incredible that the women would brag and fantasize about this night for years.

The only problem was that he didn't know three women who would let him fuck them. As a matter of fact, he didn't know one woman. It had been three months since he had a fuck, and that was with a paid hooker.

The hotel strippers were teasers, girls barely 18 years of age, aware they could make money showing their tits and pussy but not interested in putting out for free. The bitches all thought their pussies were treasure chests worth hundreds of dollars. Well, he didn't have that sort of money.

At 7:30pm, the strippers finished. The boys were out of money and discussed what to do next. That's when Alex got his idea.

Earlier that week, whilst driving his taxi, he had picked up a cute Japanese MILF and her daughter at the airport. He decided to tell the guys. He spoke in detail about their appearance, the house location, how the surrounding homes were empty and that they could be there undisturbed for hours.

142

Roy was the first to talk, "Alex, that sounds like the best fucking idea you have had this year. At home I have the masks we wore to that fancy dress party last month. We could wear them and they won't be able to identify us."

It was a unanimous, *let's go!!!*

Alex began to feel nauseous, maybe because of the drug ice and alcohol. He knew telling the men had been a terrible mistake.

What have I just put in motion?

They went to Roy's house, collected the masks and a half case of beer and drove out to the house. Roy killed the headlights when they entered the street and stopped nearby the only house with lights on. They grabbed their masks and walked towards the home. Roy looked cautiously through a window into a small living room. There was a three-seater lounge and a 50cm TV. He could see the girl and the mother. Both were in their nighties, ready for bed. Roy pointed to Phillip and said, "See if the front door is open."

He pointed to Mark, "You check the back door, then both of you come back here."

Two minutes later, both men had returned.

Mark said, "The back door is unlocked."

Roy grinned, "Awesome, let's go."

It was chaos when they entered the house. The mum was a dynamo; although tiny, she was a Kung Fu bitch. She had kicked Roy hard in the stomach and he took a few minutes to recover. She had also disabled Mark with a kick to the balls before Barry and Alex had restrained her. Alex responded with a solid fist to her nose, quietening her down. Since he was the first to control her, the men let him go first. They held her down as Alex raped her. She screamed for them to stop, unable to defend herself because of their numbers and strength.

Once Alex finished, Roy was to be next. He was very angry with the bitch. She had hurt him when she had kicked him and would pay for that. Mark and Alex held her down by the arms, her legs free now because Barry had left to join Phillip with the young girl. The mother kicked out at Roy and he smashed his fist into her face.

Her legs stopped lashing out at him.

That will keep the bitch quiet for a while.

He could see her right eye already beginning to swell; he had probably fractured her eye socket with his punch. He was a strong man and she was petite.

His erection was becoming painfully hard. He grabbed her night dress and ripped it from her body, the fabric tearing apart easily in his firm grip. Now fully naked, he admired her slender body trapped under his bulk.

***

The assault had continued for hours, each man taking turns to defile the mother and daughter in heinous ways. Roy was tired as he returned to the bedroom for his second assault upon the mother. She was semiconscious on the bed. He loomed over her, studying her body. She had many injuries; someone had bitten off her left ear, the right side of her face was an ugly palette of yellows and blacks and her right eye was swollen shut. Her torso was lacerated and bruised from multiple blows and he could see indentations revealing fractured ribs.

Despite the hours of abuse, the woman had fought bravely throughout the ordeal. Only now had she succumbed, her body battered and exhausted. She had small breasts with long nipples; he bent down and sucked the left nipple into his mouth, then bit down hard. He tasted her blood and spat the bleeding nipple onto the floor. The woman screamed, her left eye partially opened as she looked at him with hatred. He was very hard now, grabbing both her ankles in his left hand. He held her legs over his left shoulder and forced his engorged penis into her anus.

She screamed again which was just how he liked it.

He laughed at her distress and pain and drove his 115kg into her petite body with the ferocity of a jackhammer. He felt her pelvis fracture, which only intensified his orgasm as he slammed his body against her in rhythm with her screams.

Finally satiated, he called out, "Alex, it's time!"

After a moment, Alex entered the room holding a large serrated knife he had found in the kitchen. Roy grabbed a handful of the woman's hair and pushed her head down over the edge of the bed, exposing her slender neck. Alex savagely dragged the knife across her neck, causing a fountain of blood to spray against the bedroom wall.

"Give me the knife," demanded Roy and then he walked into the lounge room to see Mark on top of the young girl.

"Finish her, Mark. Alex has already dealt with the mother."

"Why me?"

Roy pulled Mark's mask from his head and said, "She has seen your face."

Mark looked down at the girl, "She's unconscious!"

"Stop being a fucking pansy and do it now, you owe me, so just stop bitching and do it!"

Mark took the knife and Roy watched as he raised it high and savagely plunged it into the young girl's chest. The strike was accompanied by the sound of steel against bone, then a softer swoosh as the knife reflected from the rib and entered her body. Roy turned and walked towards the front door, hearing that dreadful sound two more times. Roy knew he was an evil man but he was no child killer. A man had to have some values.

"Come on, guys, we're out of here. We've already stayed way too long!"

As Roy left the house, he felt remorse and disgust at what they had done. The five men had behaved like animals fuelled by the drug Ice.

He vowed never to consume crystal meth again. And he never did.

Part 7

Present Day

Wednesday 3/2/2012

Forty Four

Alex was pissed off. It had been a shit Wednesday; every day was becoming a shit day. He hated it here in Darwin, especially in summer. He only stayed here because people kept to themselves and he wanted to be as far away from Sydney as possible.

He was still haunted by the memories of the night they attacked the mother and the little girl in their home. A month after it had occurred, he left Sydney. He feared he would be caught and locked away in prison for what should have been the best years of his life. So he had fled, first to the Gold Coast, a great party city, then to Brisbane for work.

He had spent the past five years here in Darwin, running an Uber business; it paid the bills and allowed him to meet young women.

He had finished work for the day and was enjoying a schooner of beer at the Commercial Hotel. The barmaids were topless from 4:00pm - 6:00pm and he had arrived early to ensure a seat at the bar.

Evelyn was English and his favourite, just 22 years of age, with massive jugs that jiggled about like a couple of puppies when she reached for a schooner glass to pour a beer.

At the end of happy hour, Evelyn's shift had finished, so he decided to head home. He had a good buzz from the beer and wondered if he was over the limit. He couldn't afford to lose his license. He had parked in the hotel's rear car park, which was quiet at this time of night. Walking to his car, he noticed an elderly Japanese man standing nearby. Alex hated Japanese tourists, "Hey you! Nippondenso! Why don't you fuck off back to wherever it is you came from?"

The Japanese man executed a polite bow and said in perfect English with a British accent, "Mr Webster, I am pleased to meet you. I have been waiting for this day for a very long time." Then, with speed that defied his age, the man had closed the three-metre gap that separated them and hit him with a savage uppercut that snapped his head backwards. Alex's eyes rolled into his head, his legs buckled under him and his vision darkened.

The rough bump woke him. He was bound with his arms behind his back and his legs in a crouching position. It was dark. He could hear the road and realised he was in the boot of a car. The Japanese man was abducting him.

Alex was terrified, a gnawing fear permeating his thoughts. The man had said he had waited a long time. The mother he had murdered ten years ago was Japanese; could this be related? His stomach heaved and he vomited down the front of his shirt. He had read about the death of Roy Homer and Phillip Longtree.

How had this man found him?

The car stopped, the boot opened and the Japanese man lifted him out as easily as if he were a child. Alex had let himself go. His arms lacked muscle, and driving an Uber didn't give a man much of a workout. He had been drinking too much and had developed a beer belly. He knew he couldn't defend himself against this powerful man even if he weren't bound. The man carried him into an industrial building, dropping him heavily onto the oil-stained concrete floor.

What was this man's intentions?

Urine ran unnoticed down his right leg and soaked his sock.

"What do you want? I don't have much money. I will give you everything I have if you let me go."

"You will stay here for a while. I want you to reflect on the crime you committed against a defenceless mother and daughter ten years ago. I want you to experience remorse; perhaps your soul can be saved.

Tomorrow, you will meet two people who wish to settle an old debt of justice."

The Japanese man padlocked a solid iron ankle restraint on his leg. It looked like something from the time of the Spanish Inquisition. A heavy chain secured him to a large metal pillar bolted to the concrete floor.

The man reached into his jacket, removed a cotton bud and said, "Open your mouth."

Alex complied. The man swabbed his mouth, then stored the cotton bud in a Ziplock bag and returned it to his suit coat pocket.

The man cut the cable ties binding his arms and Alex felt pins and needles from the blood circulation flowing freely now after being restricted.

"I will visit you tomorrow. Use the time to reflect on your life and pray to your god for forgiveness for what you have done."

Alex surveyed his surroundings. The chain that restrained him to the pillar was about 2 metres long, manufactured from thick metal links and impossible to break. The moonshine entering through the small glass windows near the roof provided the only light in the dimly lit room. The concrete was filthy, covered in dust accumulated through years of vacancy.

Immature graffiti adorned the wall and opposite him was written: *for a good time, call Jessie 0444 343 1- -.* The last two digits were illegible due to a crude drawing of a penis ejaculating over them.

He could hear movement from the ceiling and was afraid to contemplate what evil lurked there.

The room was filled with the stench of urine and semen, which had saturated the concrete floor from years of vandals, squatters, drug taking and fucking.

He was imprisoned.

He began to cry.

He knew this was not going to end well.

Forty Five

Jodie was lying in bed. It was 1:00pm Wednesday. She felt dreadful and had vomited several times today. She hadn't eaten since lunch on Monday and she had emptied that burger into the gutter when she left that terrible house. Her mother was worried about her and hadn't gone to work today. She had encouraged her to eat some dry biscuits and drink a glass of lemonade, but it was useless. Jodie didn't want anything. Well, maybe just to die. She should die; that way, the haunting memories would be buried with her.

Her door opened and her mother entered, accompanied by two big men in paramedic uniforms. They were carrying a stretcher. Her mother said, "I'm taking you to the hospital, darling. Something is terribly wrong and I'm concerned about your health."

"I don't want to go, mum, I'm okay." One of the men lifted her arm and jabbed a needle into her shoulder. Immediately, she felt a warmth come over her, the sadness of the past days evaporated and she started to feel euphoric…then nothing.

***

Margaret, Jodie's mother, was sitting on a chair next to the bed where Jodie slept peacefully with the help of the tranquiliser that the doctor had administered. Her phone rang and seeing the caller ID, she answered,

"Hello, Sonia."

"Is Jodie ok?"

"No, she's in hospital. She hasn't eaten or drunk anything for days and the doctor has taken blood samples to analyse and hopefully determine what is ailing her."

There was a pause, and then, "Mrs Tailor, Jodie made me promise not to tell you, so you can't tell her it was me, please. On Monday, she was abducted, drugged and raped. The man recorded the rape and has threatened to publish it on the internet if she got the police involved."

Margaret felt like she had been kicked in the stomach by a horse. No wonder her beautiful little girl had been so unwell. "Can you come and see her, please, Sonia? I think she would cherish your company at this dreadful time in her life."

Margaret pressed the room buzzer and the ward nurse entered a few minutes later. She explained what Sonia had revealed. The nurse hugged her and said, "It's ok, we can help. I will contact the police. They need to be involved and I will arrange for our sexual assault counsellor to talk to Jodie before the police arrive."

Jodie woke at 2:30pm to see her mother, Sonia, and another woman she didn't know. She was in a hospital bed, an intravenous line in her wrist connected to a bag of clear fluid on a stand. The woman came over, held her hand and said, "Hello, Jodie, my name is Robin. I'm a counsellor, and I help young women recover from sexual assault." Jodie's blood went cold. They knew. Sonia had betrayed her, everyone would know and she started to cry again.

At first, it was challenging to discuss, but once she recited what had happened to her, she began to feel better. It was as though sharing the story with others lessened her burden. When she had finished, all three women were crying. Only Jodie's eyes remained dry, her crying completed over the past days. She started feeling more robust and determined to put this behind her and continue her life. She yearned for this man to be put behind bars and punished for what he did.

At 4:00pm, two police officers entered the hospital room and introduced themselves as constables Ken Richards and Beverley Hill. Beverley started, "I know this is difficult for you, Jodie but we need to take your statement before we can arrest the man who did this to you. Are you well enough for us to do that now? The sooner we get started, the quicker we can get this man off the streets."

Jodie nodded and then told the police officers what had happened. Beverley stopped her several times to ask questions, most of which she could answer. When she had finished, the male officer Ken asked her, "Do you know where he took you?"

"Yes, I caught the bus close to the house; it was Stop 203, Route 606. His house was on the opposite side of the street, the fourth house." Ken opened his iPad and spent a moment doing something, then turned the screen to face Jodie. She was looking at Google Maps Street View. He asked, "Is this the house?"

She studied the picture. Seeing the house again made her heartbeat race, her anxiety returned and she dry retched. "Yes!"

Beverley said, "Thank you, Jodie. You are a brave young lady. Next time we see you, we will have this man in custody." Then, the two police officers bid them goodbye, turned and left the room. Ken rang the chief and explained that the abducted girl knew the location where the assault had taken place and he asked permission to go to the address and apprehend this man immediately. The chief agreed and they drove to the destination.

***

They walked up the stairs to the front door. Ken knocked heavily on the door, waited 60 seconds and then knocked again, adding, "Police Officers, open the door now!" He knocked the mandatory third time, waited 60 seconds, then, using his right foot, kicked hard on the door, positioning the kick next to the lock and the door flew open. Taking their torches from their utility belts, they peered into the house. They could see that somebody was lying on the floor in the living room. They retrieved their forensic shoe booties from the car and entered the premises. Ken reached down and placed his thumb against the man's neck. He was cold and had no pulse. If this man assaulted the young girl, he would not do that again.

He rang the chief, "It's a homicide, chief. The man is naked on the floor and the body is missing its genitals and an eye. The body is cold and has no signs of rigor mortis, so he has been dead for more than a day". Ken had seen enough homicides to know that rigor mortis only lasted about 36 hours after death. "Ok, get the medical examiner and forensics out to the house. You and Beverley secure the scene and stop anyone who shouldn't be there." Then the chief hung up.

***

Peter and Kim were in the evidence room discussing their options. It was 6:30pm and they were considering going for a beer. Perhaps the alcohol would help them think of creative ways to progress and solve this case. His mobile phone rang. It was the chief.

"Hello Chief, what is it?"

"Peter, a young girl was sexually assaulted on Monday afternoon and has only reported it today. I sent two officers to get her statement and they went to the location where the assault took place. Inside was a crime scene similar to those you've been working on. The victim was naked and tortured, which could be murder number three. I want you to get out there now."

"On our way," Peter said. It didn't take them long to travel to the third victim's home in Bankstown, Sydney. They entered the lounge room where the medical examiner studied the body.

Peter carefully surveyed the crime scene. There was very little blood this time, just a small puddle where the genitals had once resided. He was naked, his legs bound and he was clearly dead; the body was the colour of flour. The victim was staring at the ceiling, one eye bulging, the other missing, just an empty eye socket remaining. He had been dead for some time as the room held that unmistakable odour of a decomposing body.

Peter said, "Hi Tom, what can you tell us?"

"Looks to be the handiwork of the same killer from your previous two cases. I'll examine the body tonight and meet you tomorrow morning in the evidence room at 9:30am."

Forty Six

Thursday 4th February

Yesterday, the chief had approved Tess to work exclusively to help solve the case and Peter had called Tess immediately, requesting she meet him and his team at 8:30am in the evidence room.

Tess was excited when she arrived. She had only worked on the periphery of investigations and now she was an active investigative team member. However, by 9:00am, she was looking very distressed. First, they had shown her photos of the three murders and then they had explained the relationship to the home invasion cold case. Finally, Peter provided a summarised version of the home invasion that had gone terribly wrong ten years ago. Not wanting to traumatise her too much, they were selective in what they told her, enough for her to get the general idea. There was no point in all of them having restless nights.

Tess was having a second coffee, her hand was shaking and her voice was unsteady when she said, "I never knew people could be so sadistic."

In his usual jovial voice, Tom said, "Good morning," as he entered the room. Peter introduced Tess to Tom and explained her role in the investigation.

Tom started, "Victim's name is Barry Shrimpton aged 31. Time of death is estimated to be Tuesday 2nd Feb between 5:00am and 11:00am. The cause of death is suffocation due to a blockage in the victim's throat and crushed windpipe. The victim's penis was severed and forced deep into his throat. The damage to the windpipe was extensive and the blood vessel damage was consistent with being struck with a metal bar. However, closer examination revealed defined bruising from a thumb and forefinger. I guessed this to be from the grip of a strong man. However, the impressions left are slender and could only be a powerful woman. I found both his testicles in his stomach, suggesting the victim was forced to swallow them whilst alive. The right eyeball was missing and not found at the crime scene; perhaps the killer had taken it."

Tess's complexion had paled and Tom paused.

"I'm fine. Please continue."

"The right eyeball socket was shattered, unable to retain the eyeball in place. I have seen similar injuries in professional boxers or victims assaulted with a heavy blunt object such as a baseball bat. This injury was unique as the surrounding area wasn't damaged, which is very unusual. It was like someone had just plucked his eye out." Tom paused for effect and the three people just looked at him, waiting for him to continue.

Peter said, "Any other injuries?"

Tom looked at Tess, then continued. "The victim's arms had been immobilised by severing the brachial plexus nerves. This requires knowledge of human anatomy. A blade had been inserted under his collarbone and had expertly severed all the nerves in both arms, rendering them ineffective. Bleeding from all the injuries was cauterised except for the blood vessels in the penile region."

Tom paused and looked at the three officers and said, "To summarise, the killer stripped him, tied his legs together, then paralysed his arms so they could torture him. They limited his blood loss so the torture could be sustained over a long period. This was a callous murder undertaken by someone who wanted this man to suffer."

Peter said, "Tom, we found photos and video of an assault on a young woman, obviously taken in his bedroom. The equipment was still in place, and the photo's metadata indicates the attack occurred between 12:30pm

- 2:30pm Monday. The computer is being examined today and I expect to find additional videos and photos of other victims. Have you run a DNA test against the crime database? I expect we'll find a match."

Tom said, "Yes, I did. I received the results this morning. They match a DNA sample taken from the mother and girl from your home invasion case. Whoever is committing these murders has killed three of the five men involved in that home invasion. I expect we'll have two more murders remaining unless we can find and stop this assassin. I have to leave now. I have a busy day with another five autopsies to perform. Please keep me informed of any progress in your investigations."

The three stood before the storyboard and Peter started, "So let's begin with what we know. First, the three men were all involved in the home invasion. Two more men remain and we don't know whether our killer knows who they are; however, since these murders have been meticulously planned, we should assume that they do."

"We have one suspect, Himari Miyagawa, who left the country on Monday afternoon after the second murder. I received an email update from the Singapore police stationed at the Marina Sands Hotel and she has not entered the room since Tuesday. Since Himari Miyagawa left before the third murder, we should assume that she was either one of several killers or a decoy. The first two murders were spectacularly staged to destroy evidence and to be found quickly. The third victim would not have been found for some time if the young girl hadn't reported her assault to the police. This is to our advantage. We need to keep the third murder confidential, with no media and no family contact until I say.

"I suspect the killer wanted us to believe there were only two killings and that they had left the country. We were to follow her decoy to Singapore, where the trail would end, allowing the killer time to continue to hunt down the remaining men. So, team, the question is, how do we relocate our killer? Tess, any ideas?"

"Yes, give me a couple of hours and I'll meet you back here at 1:00pm to brief you on what I've found."

Tess went upstairs to her desk and started her search. She logged into the Main Roads registration database and searched for any other vehicles registered in the name of Himari Miyagawa. Tess got a match to an HSV Commodore registered at the same fake address.

She logged into the Mascot Parking database and typed in the registration of the Commodore. Two minutes later, she had a response. The Commodore had entered the long-term parking area on Tuesday, 2/2/2021 at 2:30pm and had not exited. Tess remembered the medical examiner had estimated the time of death for the third victim was Tuesday morning. Himari Miyagawa had left Australia on the previous day. The HSV Commodore registered to her had entered the airport car park after she had left Australia and after the death of the third victim. It could not have been driven there by Himari Miyagawa. She realised that there must have been two people involved in the killings of these three men.

Tess's heart was racing with excitement. Her hands flew across the keyboard as she created a Python script to execute an AI facial recognition search.

Forty Seven

Alex had trouble sleeping, his mind playing terrible scenarios to him. Eventually, he did sleep restlessly, his bowels rumbling when he woke. He needed to take a shit, so he went as far from the pillar as the chain allowed and defecated on the floor like an animal. He couldn't remove his trousers from the leg that was shackled, forcing him to tear his underwear away. He used the torn underwear to wipe his bum, then threw them into a far corner.

He looked at his watch. It was 9:00am Thursday and despite spending hours trying to develop an escape plan, he hadn't come up with anything. It was getting hot within the confines of the old factory, his cell; no air was circulating. He was perspiring heavily, losing valuable moisture. His clothes were already soaked in his sweat and the day would get hotter. He was very thirsty now; he hadn't had a drink since he left the hotel yesterday.

He began to consider that he might die here, either from the heat, thirst or by the hand of the Japanese. He wondered when the Japanese man would return. He needed to pee, so he did, soaking his trousers; it felt warm against his body. He could smell the poop in the corner, his urine on his clothing. He began to sob. Then wail. Then scream.

Forty Eight

The flight from Cairns to Darwin took 2.5 hours and they arrived at 10:30am. Takeo had flown using the name from the fake passport he had used to enter Australia. Sakura had travelled as Aiko Bianchi. The symbolism of using her mother's name to dispatch her mother's killer appealed to her. She was laying down a trail of identity confusion for the police.

Waiting for them at the arrival gate was Tatsuo, the dragon man. Sakura had met Tatsuo several times while staying at her grandfather's home. He had spent hours working with them whilst they had planned their revenge on her mother's killers. He also helped finalise the logistics and obtain the necessary items for the various missions.

Tatsuo had asked her grandfather if he could be present when they located Aiko's murderer as he wanted to participate in this man's fate. He sought justice for Aiko, whom he had known since her birth. Hirutu and Mirako had gifted him the honour of being their daughter's godfather when she was a sweet little girl just five years old. Tatsuo had loved Aiko as much as her parents and he had grieved for days when he learned of her murder, saddened that he could not be there that horrendous night to protect her.

They embraced and Sakura whispered, "Do you have him?" Tatsuo looked at her and said, "Of course, little Sakura, I would have travelled to hell and back to ensure he paid for what he did to you and our beautiful

Aiko."

Tatsuo held his hand out to Takeo, who took it and then wrapped his free arm around him, pushing his body up close to him in a bear hug. It was an unusual display of affection from these men.

When the embrace ended, Tatsuo reached into his jacket breast pocket and removed an envelope which contained the DNA sample of the man they believed to be the fifth home invader. He handed it to Takeo, who put the envelope in the same pocket which held the DNA specimen from Mark Chisholm. He promised to get the results back to them by morning.

Takeo was on a 1:30 pm flight to Tokyo today, which would arrive in Tokyo at 7:30 pm tonight. A senior DNA technician would meet him to undertake the DNA testing. Once analysed and compared against the police reports of the home invasion, Takeo would confirm if the Cairns man and the man they had detained in Darwin were correct.

Takeo bent over so he could place a kiss on Sakura's cheek and said, "I will wait with high expectations to hear how Alex's final hours are spent. I hope this final death will cleanse the poison of these men from your body." He picked up his travel bag, turned and headed towards the international terminal.

Tatsuo picked up Sakura's suitcase and together, they walked out of the terminal into the oppressive heat of the Darwin summer, 95% humidity and already 38C.

Tatsuo drove Sakura to an old industrial area near the Darwin docks. At the end of the road stood a decrepit brick warehouse, surrounded by sixty metres of vacant land separating it from the other industrial buildings. It stood behind a padlocked gate and a three-metre-high chain wire fence, finished with three rows of barbed wire strung across the top. Tatsuo unlocked the gate and they drove into the concrete compound. The warehouse had a single shuttered door that opened to a loading dock. The roof was rusted tin, with a row of opaque wired glass windows just below the roof.

Sakura noticed the absence of air-conditioning units on the roof. She could feel the heat radiating off the concrete in the car park. She knew it would be very uncomfortable in that building. The roller door started to rise, the whir of a motor and rattling chain easily heard from the outside. Sakura walked towards the opening door; behind it stood her grandfather. She stepped onto the loading dock, wrapped her arms around him and kissed him on the cheek, "Hello, grandfather."

Hirutu looked down at her, smiling, "Hello Sakura, wonderful to see you. I am overwhelmed by your success. You have performed magnificently in avenging your mother and yourself from the atrocities these men inflicted on you both."

"Grandfather, I am eager to meet the man who murdered my mother."

"Come inside and I will introduce you to Alex Webster."

Forty Nine

Sakura and the others entered the room where Alex was held captive. The air was stifling hot and the room stank of faeces, sweat and fear. Her mother's killer was chained to a metal pillar and was lying on the floor. He looked to be asleep or perhaps unconscious. He didn't look too scary now, unlike the night he wore the pig mask.

Her grandfather told Tatsuo, "Please prepare him for the interview."

Tatsuo had tortured many men over the decades he had worked for Hirutu. He was exceptionally skilled in the art of torture and could keep a man alive for days if that was what was desired. They had weakened the man from heat, starvation and thirst; however, that was just the beginning. Now was the time for him to become familiar with pain.

Tatsuo organised the gear he had prepared for this special day, a significant day, a day of justice for Aiko. He attached chains to each of Alex's wrists. The chains went up to the beam overhead and over a pulley. Tatsuo pulled the chain and lifted Alex to his feet, his arms raised above his head. This position restricts the blood flow to the shoulder muscles, which, over time, becomes very painful as the ball joint is slowly pulled from the shoulder socket.

Alex awakened and screamed. His shoulders were being torn from his

163

body. He found he could ease the pain by rising onto his toes, but this was temporary, and he couldn't stand on his toes for long. The older man introduced himself. "My name is Hirutu Hotato. I am an oyabun, the leader of my family's Yakuza business. This woman next to me is my granddaughter. She was a ten-year-old girl when you and your friends brutalised her. Her mother was my only daughter, my beautiful Aiko. We know that it was you who cut her throat and took her life."

The colour drained from Alex's face, his fear prominent.

Hirutu continued, "Your friends were eager to tell us who took Aiko's life. They are all dead now; Sakura has dealt them justice. I have travelled from Tokyo to share the pleasure of seeking revenge for my daughter. Shall we begin?"

The Japanese girl moved towards him and stared into his eyes. Her eyes were black as coal, lacking any compassion. Her stare terrified him more than any man had. Her face betrayed her disgust of him. His heart raced, and fear engulfed him, like a beast it surged throughout his body. His mouth filled with gastric bile as his stomach purged its contents.

The girl removed his clothes, using a dagger to cut his trousers away from the leg with the ankle restraint. He stood there naked, humiliated and vulnerable. He hung his head.

She turned towards her grandfather, bowed her head and presented the dagger nestled across the palms of her two outstretched hands. The grandfather bowed and took the dagger. He moved towards Alex and held it up ensuring he could see its sharp edge.

"You took my only daughter and today I am seeking my revenge."

Hirutu started to cut. First, he removed Alex's nipples, then he made diagonal incisions across his chest and stomach. He kept cutting away and Alex kept screaming and begging him to stop. Each cut was about 1cm in depth, cutting through the flesh to the subcutaneous fat layer, painful and bleeding, but not severe enough to be fatal.

Once he had finished on the front, he moved to Alex's back and started cutting there. After a while, Alex passed out. When Hirutu indicated he had finished, Tatsuo lowered the chains and Alex slumped on the floor. They would leave him like that tonight and return in the morning. They left a 500ml water bottle on the floor beside the unconscious Alex. They didn't want him to die....well. not yet.

Fifty

Tess entered the evidence room just before 1:00pm. Peter and Kim stopped talking when they heard her enter the room and looked towards her, the anticipation showing on their faces. Tess's eyes wandered over towards the evidence board. She could see they had developed a further hypothesis for what may have happened whilst she was running her searches.

Tess pushed a USB stick into the PC and the wall monitor displayed two images, side by side, of a woman. At the bottom of each image was a timestamp. She turned to the men and explained what they were looking at. "The woman on the left is travelling under the name of Himari Miyagawa. This photo was taken by departure security on Monday, 1/2/2021, at Mascot International Airport when she left Australia for Singapore. The photo on the right is taken by CCTV on the long-term parking shuttle bus on Tuesday 2/2/2021 at 2:45pm."

Peter looked at Tess, "It looks like the same woman?"

"Yes, they are very similar, but there are differences. I suspect the woman on the right is the killer of your third man; the timeline stacks up."

"Do you know where she went?" Peter asked.

Tess displayed another image which showed a woman walking towards the departure gates, "This is in the domestic airport, so she flew somewhere within Australia that day. I have a Python script executing against the airport security cameras, searching for more footage. If I can identify the departure gate, I can determine the flight and destination. I'm afraid it's going to take a few more hours. I'll contact you when I have a match."

Peter left to visit the chief. He briefed him on what they had discovered so far in the investigation. He asked if they had approval for him and Kim to travel domestically to look for the woman who they thought was their killer or at least connected to their killer. The chief had approved three days and wished him good luck.

Peter rang Kim and told him to pack a bag with clothes for three days. Then he drove home to tell his wife he would be away for a few days. He ate dinner and sat at the kitchen table enjoying a glass of merlot when his mobile rang. It was Tess.

"Peter, I have her, I'm sure. A woman flew to Cairns on Tuesday afternoon. I reviewed the passenger manifest searching for Japanese tourists and there were fifteen. One of the passengers was Aiko Bianchi!" She paused.

She heard Peter let out a deep breath.

"Tess, you are brilliant!"

"I searched the airlines' databases and Aiko Bianchi left Cairns today and flew into Darwin. So perhaps victim four lived in Cairns or the surrounding area and is now deceased the fifth man living in Darwin. We may still have time to catch her."

Peter thanked Tess then rang Qantas to reserve a seat for Darwin. Unfortunately, the earliest flight he could get was at 6:00pm Friday, arriving just after midnight. Tomorrow was going to be a long day. He took out his phone and messaged Kim to advise him of their flight booking and that they should meet in the evidence room at 9:00am tomorrow.

Fifty One

Alex slowly regained consciousness, awakened by the pain. It was dreadful. He screamed out but his throat was so dry that screaming was agonising. When he saw the bottle of water, he opened it and consumed the entire contents in seconds, his thirst unquenchable.

He looked sadly at the empty bottle and decided he needed to pee. He urinated into the bottle and screwed on the lid, deciding he may need that later. He looked at his watch; it was 2:00pm Thursday. He had been held captive for almost 20 hours. The cuts on his body stung, the salt from his sweat burning as it flowed into the wounds. The sensation was similar to being attacked by a swarm of wasps. He must have over a hundred lacerations across his body.

The light started to fade, but the factory was still unbearably hot. Alex knew that when he next saw the man and granddaughter, he would plead for their mercy and tell them how sorry he was for what he did that day. It was worth a chance, although neither of them looked like people who would be merciful. He was dizzy from the oppressive heat, loss of blood, absence of food and thirst.

Night fell and nobody had come for him. He was hungry, thirsty and terrified. That was when he decided it was time to drink the urine he had kept earlier in the afternoon, his thirst overriding his disgust. He took a small mouthful, the liquid warm and salty. He held it in his mouth but couldn't swallow it. His stomach gave an involuntary spasm and he dry retched and spat it out. He attempted another mouthful and this time he managed to keep it down.

Throughout the evening, he sipped slowly from the bottle. Later, after consuming all the urine, he pissed in the bottle again, the colour a very dark yellow. He was becoming severely dehydrated. He started to sob, then broke down and whined like a child. He had had some low times in his life, but never like this. He was trapped, like an animal. He hoped the Japanese man would return for him and he didn't care what he would do. He needed food and water.

Sleeping was difficult. Alex's chest and back were on fire from the cuts. His weakened state was allowing infection to take hold. He could hear scraping against the concrete floor. He wasn't sure what was making the sound but it terrified him.

That's when he felt a bite on his foot. Then another. Then another.

Something furry ran along his leg and bit down hard on his scrotum. He screamed in pain and jumped to his feet. He reached down with his hand and grabbed the furry body of a giant rat tearing at his scrotum. Its teeth had penetrated his testicle and arrows of pain shot into his stomach. The rat increased the pressure and Alex let loose a blood-curdling scream as he reached down and pulled at the rat. It was firmly attached to his genitals. He wrapped his thumb and first finger around its throat to strangle it. The rat continued its vicious assault on his scrotum. Alex almost fainted from the dreadful pain of his crushed and pierced testicle. Finally, he felt a slight subsidence in pressure on his testicle as the teeth receded; yanking hard, he pulled the rat from his body. He held it up to his face to study it. The room was dimly illuminated by a half-moon as the small windows limited the light. It was enough though for Alex to see the giant rat chewing ferociously, its cheeks bulging from its pointy face as it devoured the section of his scrotum that had torn from him when the rat detached. Its beady red eyes gave it a demonic appearance and he could see tiny droplets of glistening blood falling from its whiskers as it chewed. He smashed its head against the steel pillar three times, making sure it was dead and threw it against the wall.

He could see and smell dozens of rats, their beady eyes reflecting the moonlight. They were in an arc about a metre from where he stood, watching him, less confident now after watching the demise of their leader. Some peeled away to feed upon the new fare he had provided. Others chose to attack him, revelling in the thought of such a feast.

They ran up his legs. They were all over him, biting him. One bit deeply into his buttock cheek. He reached down, grabbed it and pulled. The rat refused to release its grip, so he yanked as hard as he could and tore the rat from his body, its mouth full of his flesh. He let loose another piercing scream from the pain. He held the rat steady with one hand and tore its head from its body with the other.

"You want to eat me!" he yelled, "I will eat you!"

He bit down on the smelly creature, pulling a mouthful of flesh from its body. He grabbed another rat, running up his legs and before it could get a grip, Alex broke its neck, and threw it across the room. Its mates decided it was safer to eat a relative than this man fighting back.

Alex got very little sleep that night. The rats kept returning. He quenched his thirst and hunger with the blood and flesh of these rodents.

Fifty Two

Friday 5th February

Peter was staring at the timeline on the evidence board. He had added another box to indicate a fourth victim, no name, just a location, Cairns. It was just a hypothesis for now, but it was very probable. He sat back and, releasing a deep sigh, pondered the information.

Who is this woman? If I'm correct, she has killed four men. The first, Roy Homer, was just over two weeks ago. This week, she killed Phillip Longtree on Monday and Barry Shrimpton on Tuesday. All of whom had been involved in the Bianchi home invasion ten years ago. She may have killed the fourth home invader on Wednesday in Cairns. Three men in three days!

Why the gap of two weeks between these three men and Roy?

Was it a different person? His brow wrinkled as he tried to understand what the evidence was telling him. Now, she had travelled to Darwin, which he assumed was where she would kill the fifth home invader. He was concerned that they might not arrive in Darwin in time. It would be late tonight when their flight landed. They didn't even know where to start looking for her or what name she would be using. Darwin was a small city with only 130,000 people but big enough to make it difficult to find her.

The remainder of Friday was spent obtaining a court order to detain the woman travelling under the name of Aiko Bianchi. Tess had contacted all international airlines departing Cairns, informing them of the arrest warrant for Aiko Bianchi and that she should be detained by airport security if she tried to board a flight. The authorities were also to arrest anyone travelling with her and to contact Tess when done.

Peter and Kim had contacted all the major hotels to see if any had reservations in Aiko Bianchi's name but had drawn a blank. It looked like it was back to the old-fashioned way, wearing down shoe leather. They would visit each hotel and show the photo of the suspected killer to hotel staff. Darwin had thirty-two popular hotels; if they split up, they could visit sixteen each. Hopefully, they would have better luck and the hotel staff would recognise her.

Fifty Three

Alex woke as he was hoisted onto his feet again, his arms held painfully above him, his shoulders screaming out in pain. His chest and back were on fire from the infection raging through the cuts and rat bites. Today, they had attached an ankle restraint to his free leg, chained to another steel pillar. His arms were outstretched their full length above his head and he was hoisted so high that only the tips of his toes were touching the floor. With his legs chained to opposite pillars, he was unable to move.

He cried out for them to forgive him for his actions, "I am terribly sorry. I have lived with nightmare memories of that night for ten years. I wish I could change what happened that night." The grandfather looked across at Sakura and said in Japanese, "Do you think he is remorseful? Do you think he has genuine regrets?"

Sakura said, "He has only suffered for two days, I will suffer for a lifetime. I cannot forgive him. Grandfather, I will let you have the honour of delivering his Justice."

Earlier that morning, Takeo had confirmed that the DNA samples for Mark Chisholm and Alex Webster matched the Police file DNA samples. They had found all five men.

Sakura took her tantō from the bundle she had carried into the room and handed it to her grandfather. The tantō is often used in the Seppuku ceremony when a warrior decides to die with honour and by their own

173

hand. Hirutu unsheathed the tantō and walked towards Alex. He said in perfect English, "I do not forgive you for taking my daughter's life. A life for a life is your punishment!" Then he pushed the sword's point into Alex's abdomen, just above his pubic bone. The blade easily penetrated his body to a depth of 20 cm. Alex screamed, "No! No! Please stop!"

Hirutu placed both his hands on the hilt of the sword and, using his strong arms, slowly drew it upwards, all the way to Alex's breastbone. The beautifully crafted blade was as sharp as a razor and the steel was strong. It opened Alex's belly like a zipper. Hirutu withdrew the sword and Alex's entrails slipped from his body, falling to the floor. Some remained suspended against his legs.

Alex's screams had increased in volume during the upward cut, which is known to be incredibly painful. Over the centuries, samurai who endured the pain of the Seppuku ceremony for two minutes or more before signalling to their second it was time to sever their head and end the pain had become legendary. Unfortunately, for Alex, he didn't have a second to end his pain. He would endure it until the Japanese decided he had paid his debt.

The three stood silently watching the fatally injured man screaming in pain, the realisation of his fate etched deeply in his facial features. When Sakura was satisfied he had suffered enough and before he lost consciousness, she stood before him and said, "Alex, I do not forgive you for what you did that night. I curse you to live your afterlife in purgatory." She reached into his chest cavity with her right hand and ripped Alex's beating heart from his body. She held the pulsating heart up so he could see it. For a fleeting moment, before his eyes clouded over and his head sunk to his chest, she saw his life drain from his tortured features.

The man who had worn the pig mask was finished. The three left the complex, padlocking the loading dock roller door and the gate. They had paid six months' rent for the factory complex and it would be some time before Alex's body was found. They would be safely back home in Tokyo, far from the Australian authorities. They climbed into the rental car and drove back to their hotel.

Fifty Four

Sakura returned to the hotel and removed the jar labelled *Mr Pig* from her backpack. She studied it, observing the heart lying silently in the liquid. This final symbolic act calmed her mind and she felt relaxed and satisfied. Alex had killed her mother and broken her heart; now she had his.

Finally, she had avenged her mother and could now focus on the rest of her life. For the past decade, she had been consumed with grief and was seeking revenge. She had trained hard so she could be the best she could be. She had killed all five of the men who had ruined her life.

That night, she dined with her grandfather and Tatsuo. They ate lobster and abalone, each dish an expensive delicacy in Japan. Her grandfather bought the most expensive bottle of French Champagne in the hotel cellar and the three toasted Aiko together. It was a happy moment for the family. At the end of the meal, Sakura bowed to her grandfather, then turned to Tatsuo and said, "Goodnight. I will see you in the morning for our sightseeing trip."

Sakura left the dining area and walked through the hotel to the tour desk. A young man was seated behind the counter, reading a book. He looked up as she approached, smiled and asked how he could help her. "I would like to book the all-day cruise to Southwest Vernon Island for three adults tomorrow, please." He typed the information into his computer and, after 30 seconds, said, "No problem, I can do that. It's a great choice; it's our most popular day trip. The shuttle bus will collect you at the entrance at 9:00am and return around 6:00pm. The cost is $960." Sakura said, "I would like to book it to my room please." The travel clerk printed off the invoice, handed it to Sakura, who wrote down her room, Suite 202, gave her name as Aiko Bianchi and signed the invoice.

That night was the best sleep Sakura had had in a decade. She dreamt of good times with her mother. She hoped that the nightmares were gone, never to return.

Fifty Five

Saturday 6th February

Peter met Kim downstairs for a buffet breakfast at 7:30am. Last night, Tess had emailed them each a list of hotels to visit to see if they could locate the woman. The list was organised by location, so the hotels on the top of their list were the closest and the hotels towards the end of the list were the furthest away.

They had rented two vehicles at the airport when they arrived so they could separate and cover more ground. At 8:30am, they left the hotel and went in different directions to work through the list. It was frustrating for the detectives; typically, more junior officers would undertake this activity. They had been unsuccessful in obtaining approval to use local resources, so they were on their own. Each hotel visited started the same way: introductions; have you seen this woman? She may be travelling with other people...

At 11:30am at the MGM Grand Casino Hotel reservations desk, Peter Reynolds smiled. The hotel clerk had confirmed that the woman in the photo was staying at the hotel. She looked down at her PC and said, "She is staying under a reservation booked by Mr Turisomo for three rooms. They checked in on Thursday and they are checking out on Tuesday. Last night, Miss Aiko Bianchi purchased tickets from the hotel Information and Reservations Centre for a cruise to Southwest Vernon Island. They left at 9:00am this morning and are expected to return tonight around 6:00pm." Peter thanked her and asked that she not mention his visit to anyone.

Peter rang Tess and provided an update and she told him that she had no further information on the woman. It was like she had disappeared. Next, he rang the Darwin Chief of Police to advise that they had located the suspects for three murders and potentially two more. He said, "Yes, I understand, your office has briefed me."

"We expect these suspects to return to the hotel at 6:00pm. Could we have five officers from 3:00pm?"

"I will supply five of my best people. Where will they meet you?" Peter gave his hotel address. He thought two hours should be adequate to brief and prepare for the arrest with the officers, allowing an hour to return to the casino and take up the agreed positions.

Excitedly, he rang Kim, and when he answered, Peter said, "The girl is staying at the MGM Grand Casino Hotel with two older Japanese men. The hotel clerk described one man as strong and heavily tattooed and the other man's demeanour had frightened her. She described him as ruthless, cunning and not someone you would not want to get on the wrong side of!

"Kim, I'm certain these are the killers. We should be able to arrest them this evening when they return from a day trip. I was hoping you could wait in the hotel foyer in case they arrive early. I don't want you to engage with them, just wait until I come with the cavalry. Keep them under observation and notify me if they leave the hotel. Be careful with these people, Kim, they are dangerous! Deadly dangerous! I'm returning to my hotel room to prepare for the briefing with the Darwin police. I'll lay out all the photos we've collected during the case. They need to understand the type of people they will arrest this evening. I hope seven of us is enough".

Fifty Six

By 5:00pm, the police officers had taken their positions in the foyer and near the hotel entrance doors. It was now 7:00pm and the three suspects had not returned from their day trip. Peter walked to the check-in desk clerk for the third time that evening and asked if he could access the woman's room to look around.

The clerk said, "I will call the hotel manager, sir."

The hotel manager's name badge declared him as Roger and he wasn't pleased about this request and the intrusion on his guests. Once Peter had shown him the restraining order, he relented and said he would allow it only on the provision that he accompany them.

Roger used his master key to open the door to Suite 202. Peter walked in and looked around. The suite was spacious and luxurious for Darwin. It included a separate lounge area, a bath and shower, a large king-size bed and a 4x2 metre balcony with ocean views. Peter opened the wardrobe and saw that it was empty. He looked for luggage but there was none. His heart sank. He knew immediately that the other rooms would be the same. They had gone.

The cruise they had booked had been a decoy and they had extended the room reservations to give the impression that they would be here longer. Who were these people? They had the resources to travel from Japan and the logistics necessary to murder these five men. He was confident that five men had been murdered despite only finding three

179

bodies, well, partial bodies.

That's when he noticed the envelope on the bedside dresser addressed to him. Inside the envelope were two keys and a note. The calligraphy of the message flowed magnificently, the black ink of the brush strokes contrasting with the rice paper's whiteness. He held it to the light, admiring the delicate swirls and thin lines. It was beautiful and reminded him of more ancient times, a time when Buddhist monks ruled.

He shook his head. *Get a hold of yourself, Peter.* Then he read the note.

Dear Mr Reynolds,

By now, you know that I have been avenging a great injustice. Five men have finally paid their debt for the atrocities they committed on two innocent women. This burden was left to me, as the authorities were unable to apprehend these men. I have left evidence in two safety deposit boxes, one in Darwin and the other in Sydney. These can be accessed by the keys included and the information should enable you to close that home invasion case.

Please ensure Shane Edwards is updated. I know he tried his best to locate and charge these men. I'm hoping that now he can have closure as well.

Yours truly,

Innocent Assassin

xxx

Fifty Seven

Sakura slid out from under the bed covers and walked towards the breakfast nook to boil the jug and prepare a cup of tea. It was Saturday morning and they were heading home today. She felt energised. A burden had been lifted from her shoulders.

She finished her tea and was in the gym by 6:00am. She had neglected her training regime over the past week and was determined to start again today. For ninety minutes, she pressed weights, ran on the treadmill and did intensive kata sequences.

Afterwards, she showered and went down to the dining room for breakfast. She ate a simple meal of rice, porridge and fruit. She thought that Australian food was starting to make her put on weight.

Her grandfather and Tatsuo joined her before she had finished. It felt nice to share breakfast with them. This simple act solidified their relationship and their experience had created a lifetime bond.

Her grandfather said, "I have organised airport transport for 10:00am and our flight is at 1:00pm."

Sakura waited at the hotel entrance for the shuttle to take them on their day tour. A multi-coloured minivan pulled up to the Grand Hotel entrance. Sakura walked to the minivan. The door opened and the young driver leaned over and said, "Aiko Bianchi party?" His hair was dark with lengthy braids; he was unshaven and wearing a rainbow-coloured knitted cap. Something more akin to apparel worn in Jamaica. She smiled and

181

said, "Unfortunately, we must cancel. I'm sorry we wasted your time."

"Cancelling this late means you will only be refunded 20% of your payment fee."

"Tell your company to give the refund to you; it's my gratuity to you." She smiled, turned and walked back into the hotel to finalise her preparations for travelling to the airport. Behind her, she heard the young man call out, "Thank you, I appreciate it."

Sakura looked out from the window of the rental car, admiring the city of Darwin on their way to the airport. They had stopped at the Commonwealth Bank and Sakura went to the safe custody box to deposit the two jars—one containing the genitalia of Mark, the other Alex's heart. Tatsuo had arranged the safety deposit box earlier when he had arrived in Darwin. Once outside the bank, she dropped two safety deposit box keys into a kerbside bin. She wouldn't need these again. One key was for the Sydney box, the other for the Darwin box. She had left two spare keys in the envelope at the hotel for Detective Reynolds to use.

Sakura had booked her flight using the passport she had obtained in the Four Seasons Hotel Cafe in Sydney under the name Nimiko Nakamura. It was a valid passport with a valid visa. The immigration officer looked at her, looked at the passport photo and visa, and then stamped the page.

Fifty Eight

Monday 8th February

Peter and Kim were waiting at the bank entrance when the doors opened and a young bank clerk welcomed them in. They showed their badges and asked to speak to the manager. It was a woman in her forties who introduced herself as Karen. "How can I help you?"

Peter said, "We want to open a safety deposit box, number 3122. We have the key. We believe the contents could prove useful in resolving a homicide."

Karen's mouth opened slightly, "Of course, follow me." She took them to an elevator. The simple control panel consisted of just two buttons, one arrow indicating *up* and the other *down* She pressed *down* and they descended. The doors opened, revealing a short corridor with a white tiled floor and beige-coloured plasterboard on the walls. At the end of the hall was a door with a pin-pad; Karen keyed in a six-digit code and they entered. The room was sparse, with just a table and two chairs on either side. On the walls from floor to ceiling were different-sized doors, each numbered. The larger custody doors were waist-high. Security box 3122 was chest-high on the right wall. Peter inserted his key, and the door sprung open. He removed the metal box and placed it on the table, inserted the key and paused, looking at Kim, wondering what they would find. Then he opened the box.

Inside were two screw-top jars, each containing fluid and a body part. The jars were labelled using the same calligraphy style as the note left in the room. One jar was labelled *Mr Mouse* and held a man's genitals. The other was marked *Mr Pig* and contained a heart.

The metal box also contained two manilla folders. Closer examination revealed them to be copies of the original police reports on the home invasion of Aiko and Sakura Bianchi, including their respective medical examiner and hospital reports. Peter opened the police reports and flicked through the pages. He found the page that had been altered in the Aiko Bianchi report, the DNA summary. Names had been recorded against all five assailants, three of whom he recognised. They were all dead.

He showed Kim, "These people have access to our records. No wonder it's been difficult to catch them." They gathered up the evidence and returned to the hotel room. That night, they would fly back to Sydney.

Fifty Nine

Wednesday 10ᵗʰ February

Peter, Kim, Tess, Tom, Shane and the chief were assembled in the evidence room around a table on which five jars were neatly marked, each containing a gruesome specimen. The previous day, Peter and Kim had retrieved three additional jars from a second safety deposit box in Sydney. The jars held a tongue, an eyeball and a testicle. Tom had collected DNA samples from all five jars for urgent analysis against the DNA Crimes database. Peter was the first to speak. He looked at Tom and said, "What can you tell us?"

"The DNA tests returned positive for the five assailants in that home invasion. Each jar contains a different man's anatomy. This killer has found all of them."

Tess held up the jar labelled *Mr Pig* and said, "Why the strange names on the jars?"

Shane said, "The men were wearing masks: a wolf, a duck, a mouse, a pig and a weird-looking mask, which I assume is marked as *Goofy*. Not only has the killer been able to locate the men, but they have also been able to identify the mask each man was wearing."

Peter said to Tess, "What did you find out yesterday?"

"I used the two new names in the altered reports to run a police check and both came up with prior charges."

"Two years ago, Mark Chisholm had an attempted rape charge reduced to assault against a woman in Daintree. Yesterday, I contacted the local police, and they went to his home but he wasn't there. They contacted his employer, Svenson Logistics, a trucking company delivering fresh goods from the Cairns docks to local supermarkets. The office clerk confirmed he left work on Tuesday, 2/2/2021. Wednesday was his day off and he hasn't returned. It fits the timeline for the person calling themselves Aiko Bianchi who flew into Cairns Tuesday night.

"The other man was Alex Webster, convicted of a DUI charge 18 months ago in Darwin. I contacted the local police and they confirmed he wasn't home. Alex is an Uber Driver, so I contacted Uber who confirmed that he hasn't had any fares since 2:00pm Wednesday 3rd February."

Tess said, "This is a bit odd as Aiko Bianchi didn't arrive in Darwin until Thursday, so perhaps there was more than one killer, or they had an accomplice. I have advised both precincts that we suspect these men may be victims of a possible homicide and to inform me if the bodies are located."

Kim gave a little chuckle, "Possible homicide? I reckon the guy whose heart we have in this jar isn't walking around and the guy missing his fishing tackle is probably not in the best of health either."

Tess smiled and said, "Yes, I was being cautious with my wording."

Shane had been looking through the police report. He said, "I don't remember any of these men being suspects during our investigation. I don't understand how the killer could find them when we spent months sifting through different scenarios." Peter handed Shane the note he had collected from the bedside table in the MGM Casino suite. As Shane read the message, tears flowed down his cheeks. He looked at Peter and tried to speak but choked on the words.

Tess walked to Shane and put her arm around him. "It's finally over. The case is solved."

The chief looked at Peter and said, "Any leads as to who killed these three men?"

Peter shook his head and said, "No. We have nothing." The chief stood. "Well, in that case, we should put this investigation on hold. Off the record, I'm glad these men are gone. I don't want to spend more resources finding their killer. Let's solve the cases we can and get justice for those who deserve it."

Sixty

Tom was sitting in Cafe 21, situated in the eastern wing of the hospital he had visited all those years ago when Sakura was recovering. He had contacted the head nurse, Natasha Williams, who had cared for Sakura. They agreed to meet here for coffee. Whilst he waited he observed two nurses sitting at another table. They were drinking coffee and having a very animated conversation. He could only hear snippets. It sounded like they were sharing their experiences of a troublesome elderly male patient.

Then he noticed the female nurse enter the cafe and immediately recognised her. It was Natasha. She had gained a few kilograms, yet the additional weight gave her a more matronly appearance. He stood as she walked towards the table. They shook hands and sat down. A waitress took their order: a long black for Tom, a skinny latte, no sugar for Natasha. Tom studied her face as they made small talk, waiting for their drinks. It was a kind face, one that had comforted many children over the years. Her experiences had aged her, evident in the silver strands through her hair and the deepening creases radiating from the corners of her eyes. Tom knew he had aged more, and she had shown surprise at his appearance.

The coffee arrived and Natasha said, "So Tom, why did you want to meet after all these years?"

"There's been a breakthrough in the Sakura Bianchi cold case and I thought you would like to know. Do you remember Sakura?"

"Of course I remember her; it was horrible what happened to that beautiful little girl!"

Tom continued, "The police have identified and confirmed all five perpetrators through DNA testing."

"When will they be charged?" enquired Natasha.

"There won't be any charges laid. They're all dead."

"All of them? That's so unfair. They should have served life sentences for what they did to that family. How did they die?"

"Only three have been found. They were tortured and suffered horrific injuries before being killed. The person responsible has provided body parts for the remaining two who we expect have suffered a similar fate."

Natasha was processing this information when her face unconsciously lit up. Tom smiled as well.

He said, "We don't know who did it and the case has now been closed. There will be no further investigation and the killer or killers will probably never be found."

"Thank you for contacting me and telling me of this outcome, Tom. I really appreciate it." She stood and so did Tom. It was awkward until he put his arms around her, hugging her into his body. He thought he smelled apples; it was her perfume and he felt the softness of her breasts against his chest.

He whispered, "I'm so glad it's over now and Sakura can have peace. Unfortunately, she'll never know since we can't contact her as she has a new confidential identity."

"Hopefully, she's put it all behind her," responded Natasha.

She decided she wouldn't share that she knew Sakura's location and had been in contact with her for ten years. She didn't understand why she withheld this information; it just seemed like the right decision.

Sixty One

Three Months Later

Natasha parked her car in the garage, pressing the *close* button on the remote as she walked down her driveway to the letterbox. She removed the letters, probably bills, and walked back to the house. Entering the kitchen, a glance at the clock on the microwave revealed it was 9:00pm. It had been a long day, another twelve-hour shift.

I'm getting too old to keep doing this.

She could feel the varicose veins throbbing in her legs. She placed the mail on the table and went to the refrigerator. Inside was a Domino's Pizza box. She opened it and examined the three remaining pieces from her meal two nights ago. She thought that would do for tonight's dinner. She placed the box on the kitchen bench, returned to the refrigerator, removed a half-empty bottle of Sauvignon Blanc and poured herself a full glass. Taking a large sip, she savoured the wine's dryness and fruity taste. She placed the wine glass next to the mail, put the pizza in the microwave, closed the door and selected a cooking time of two minutes at 70% power.

Sitting at the kitchen table, she sorted the mail and noticed the grey envelope. It was made from rough paper and her address had been written in the elegant handwriting she immediately recognised as Sakura's. It was the tenth letter she had received over the past decade and she had watched the script mature in quality from that of a child to an adult. Each year, the letters were richer in their content and she had marvelled at the improvement in Sakura's physical and mental health.

Clearly, her grandfather's decision to send her to the Sohei Temple to learn the secrets of this ancient martial arts lifestyle had been instrumental in her development. Each letter had become lengthier, the last letter spanning twenty pages. Natasha's letters were more straightforward; her life was one of an unchanging routine. Her content focussed more on complimenting Sakura on her achievements at the temple. She knew it would be a year before Sakura read her accolades, yet she imagined Sakura would enjoy the dialogue despite the delay.

This letter was short, just half a page and dated four months prior. She began to read.

Dear Natasha, I hope this letter finds you well. I graduated from the temple and am now a Sohei Warrior. I will be leaving the temple today and returning to the normal world. I am both excited and apprehensive as it's been so long. Life here has been simple and life back in the real world will be noisy with many people. Unfortunately, this will be my last letter to you as I need to ensure my location is secretive for reasons I cannot tell you. Over the years, I have enjoyed reading your letters as you were my only contact with Australia and the world, outside of Japan. I am so grateful that I was fortunate to have you nurture me through those early months in the hospital as I lay in bed crying many nights, wishing I had died with my mother. Having your support and love carried me through those dark days. My body has fully healed and I am powerful and flexible due to countless hours of training and exercise. My mind has matured and recovered through a decade of meditation and tuition by the holy monks. Yet my heart is still mourning my mother. To fully heal, I must avenge her and then I will be complete.

It is my destiny.

Love, Sakura xxx

Ding! sounded the microwave, announcing that the pizza was ready. A tear rolled down Natasha's cheek.

Good on you, Sakura! Now you are complete.

She stood, replaced the letter in the envelope and placed it in the drawer with the other nine envelopes containing ten years of correspondence. She removed the pizza from the microwave, sat at the table and took a bite of the hot, cheesy meal. Then she took a long sip of her wine.

She smiled. Today had ended up being a very good day!

Epilogue

Sakura had been lying on the bench for four hours and the tattooist was finishing up. He cleaned the tattoo with a clear liquid from a squeeze bottle and wiped it with a cloth. The new ink shone brilliantly, the colours vivid.

Now she had five ribbons. Keong, the tattooist, had suggested he tattoo using the traditional Japanese Tabori style. She agreed and he also re-inked the other three ribbons to ensure the colours matched. He added a kaiken, a Japanese dagger, as background.

Sakura walked to the mirror and smiled, happy with the result. The ink looked incredible and the design was superb, better than she could have hoped for. She was proud of the way her breasts framed the tattoo and how it hid her scars. She was a woman, an attractive woman, and she was a warrior! She was finally starting to feel comfortable with her body.

That night when she had finished eating dinner with her grandparents, Mirako said, "Sakura, I have some items Hirutu and I retrieved from your home in Sydney that we thought you would want." She got up and walked over to a side table on which sat a beautifully crafted wooden chest. She brought it to the dining table and placed it gently in front of Sakura.

The chest was constructed from polished cherry wood and inlaid with small pieces of abalone shells forming a Peony flower pattern. The hinges were polished brass, as was the latch that held the lid closed. It was magnificent, obviously handmade by a master craftsman. Sakura opened the chest and inside were two more boxes constructed of the same materials and every bit as exquisite as the chest that held them.

She removed the first, opened it, and inside, lying on a red silk lining, were three pieces of her mother's jewellery. She lifted a gold necklace with a heart-shaped locket from the box. She opened the locket to reveal a photo of her father and, on the opposite side, a picture of a very young Sakura.

Also inside the box was a wooden hair comb inlaid with a swirling pattern of abalone shell. The last piece was a golden bracelet in the shape of a serpent. It was stunning and delicate, the head of the serpent finished with two sapphires for eyes. Sakura knew that these were all gifts from her father to her mother. She held each piece in her hands, holding the precious items gently, not wanting to damage them.

She replaced them in their box and removed the second box. Inside were two delicate ceramic Japanese teacups, one with the pattern of a red dragon wrapped around its outside. The other was surrounded by a design of Peony flowers. She remembered the name of the flowers now. The glue her mother had used to repair the teacup had aged and discoloured with time, emphasising the breaks. Her heart started to ache as she remembered the morning she had accidentally dropped and broken the cup. She remembered how her mother had looked as she kneeled on the floor collecting the pieces whilst comforting Sakura that it was okay. It was just a cup.

The last item in the box was a photo album. Sakura gently removed it and opened it to the first page. There was only one photo on this page, her parents' wedding photo. She studied the picture, her mother so beautiful in a white silk Japanese kimono, her father in a smart white suit with a white top hat. She was only eight when her father died and she now realised that her memory of him had grown dimmer. She had forgotten how handsome he had been. Peering at her mother, she realised that her memory of Aiko was also fading.

She turned the page and looked at a photo of her mother lying in a hospital bed, her father, with an enormous smile, standing next to the bed holding a tiny newborn. Her mother was smiling into the camera yet looking drawn after the trauma of childbirth. Sakura's eyes filled with tears and her vision began to blur. She closed the album and replaced all the items in the chest.

These gifts were priceless; she would cherish them forever. She moved around the table, wrapped her arms around her grandmother's neck, kissed her cheek and said, "Thank you, these gifts have made me so happy. I love you both and am grateful to live here with you. I feel revived and ready to start my new life."

Her grandfather said, "Sakura, it has come to my attention that a rogue group of Yakuza in Osaka is trafficking young girls into prostitution. Some of these girls are only ten years of age. My cousin contacted me; he sounded very distressed. His niece has been kidnapped and he thinks these men have taken her. I have obtained the name of this group's oyabun (the leader) using my connections. Would you be interested in helping me resolve this kidnapping, punish these men and shut down their operation?"

Sakura Bianchi's story continues in Book 2.

'Innocent Girls'

Here is an extract

Day six since the abduction
<u>1</u>

Sakura sat in the rear seat of the sedan provided by her grandfather, Hirutu. He was the oyabun (leader) of the Hirutu yakuza. The car had been stolen three weeks earlier and tonight, the registration plates had been replaced with those from another vehicle. These precautions were necessary to avoid detection from the police and the Hidetada yakuza family, who were the most prominent human trafficking syndicate in Japan.

Tonight, they were visiting a baishun yado (brothel) to begin searching for a young girl who had been abducted six days earlier to be forced into prostitution. They didn't know exactly where she was being held but they suspected the Hidetada yakuza was involved and they knew this baishun yado was connected to them.

Two of her grandfather's most trusted and senior men sat in the front seat. Tatsuo Ishikawa was driving. He was of average height for a Japanese man but very powerful and trained daily. He had broad shoulders, a thick neck and a powerful chest. Despite being in his early sixties, he was still a formidable warrior and many younger men would think twice before confronting him. Tatsuo means 'Dragon Man' in Japanese. So, when Sakura first met him at her grandfather's home, she thought it an applicable name as his body was covered entirely in colourful yakuza-style tattoos, except for his head, neck, and hands.

In the front passenger seat sat Takeo Kobayashi. He was big for a Japanese man, standing over 200 centimetres tall and weighing 105kg, all muscle. He had a scar running from his right ear lobe to just below his jaw, an old wound from a knife fight with two older men when he was only 14. Takeo means 'Warrior' in Japanese; that was also a very fitting name.

Yakuza have an unwritten code - not to interfere with another family's business as this creates tension and conflict. Twenty-three years ago, the Hidetada yakuza decided they would control all of Tokyo's prostitution assets and went to war with other yakuza clans involved in prostitution. The battle had raged for six months and, at its conclusion, one hundred and fifty men had lost their lives. The police force obtained significant budget increases to halt the conflict and prevent the death of innocent bystanders. Three hundred baishun yados had been shut down and revenues for all yakuza clans dropped dramatically as clients stopped buying services. Over four hundred yakuza were arrested and imprisoned. It had taken a decade for the businesses to be re-established and profitable.

Sakura's grandfather remembered the war well since his businesses were also targeted. It was important that tonight his team not be identified as the Hirutu family yakuza. He did not want Hidetada to know they were searching for the girl and he did not want to start another conflict.

Sakura activated Bluetooth on her phone and connected it to the car's audio system. She played the audio message her grandfather had provided as they left his house. It described the layout of the baishun yado they would visit tonight. The audio recording had been obtained through blackmail, a common tactic used by the yakuza. They had obtained a video of an important man in compromising positions with a woman who was part of their yakuza family. They had asked her to seduce the man and record it without the man's knowledge. Once she understood why they needed the video, she was happy to help in the investigation. They also had a video of the man entering and leaving the baishun yado they were visiting tonight. They had threatened to provide this footage to his wife who was unaware of his nocturnal activities. The audio played through the car speakers, the voice that of a distressed man.

"The door is protected by two video cameras monitored by guards in an office on the first floor. Both guards carry handguns and knives. Two heavy latches secure the thick door; it would be difficult to breach it forcefully. The door opens into a small vestibule and stairs lead to the first floor. Halfway up the stairs, there is a small landing where the stairs change direction and lead up to the first floor in the opposite direction. A corridor runs to the end of the building. All the rooms are accessed on the right side of the corridor. There are two bedrooms. A third room is where the guards are stationed and the fourth is a small bathroom with a shower. When a client arrives, one guard will go downstairs to let them in, take the cash and lead them to one of the two rooms depending on the type of woman the man has requested. They are warned not to injure the girls or there would be serious consequences. These men are big, ugly and professional thugs."

The audio finished and the three-person team discussed their strategy while nearing their destination. The baishun yado was in an older area of Tokyo which consisted of traditional buildings from the 1900s. Paper lanterns hung from most of the wooden shop fronts. All the shops were small, just two levels, and made from timber. Some were painted, others had allowed the timber to be exposed to the elements and the wood had turned a grey silver over time. The signage on the buildings was brightly painted or used lighting to advertise their names. The original homes and shops had been converted into restaurants and geisha bars, interspersed with several high-end baishun yados.

They drove slowly past their destination. Sakura looked at the building, checked it against the photo on her phone and was satisfied it was the correct business. Tatsuo drove for another block and then parked the car.

2

Sakura took hold of her tsurugi sword and her tantō (a short, bladed sword), pulled the mask of the ninja hood down to hide her face, with just her eyes showing, and then stepped out of the car. Once outside, she stored the swords in their sayas (scabbards), which had been sewn into the back of her outfit, only the sword hilts showing. Then, together the three of them walked to the baishun yado.

They passed by a karaoke bar and music drifted outside with the sounds of a drunken crowd. The night air was calm and crisp. There was a rumble of thunder in the distance. A storm was threatening. The street was poorly lit as the local businesses had resisted the council's initiative to install street lighting. Instead, they preferred the illumination from their establishments, retaining this ancient town's cultural aspects. Unfortunately, this resulted in pockets of darkness lingering at the fringes of the light.

Walking towards the baishun yado, they were startled by a deep meow. A black cat emerged from the darkness, walked directly across their path, raised its tail, and sprayed them, a tomcat's act of defiance. Sakura wasn't superstitious or religious. She learned about the world's reality at the young age of ten when, during a home invasion, she was sexually assaulted, left for dead and orphaned. Regardless, she couldn't help but think the cat's appearance was an ominous symbol.

They studied the baishun yado. They could see the two cameras on either side of the door, providing a view of anyone standing there. However, by staying close to the wall, they could remain out of the camera's range. So Sakura and Takeo took positions on either side of the door directly under the cameras.

Tatsuo walked towards the door, his head slightly down. He wore a wide-brimmed kasa (hat) to hide his face from the camera as he knocked on the door. When they heard the door bolt being withdrawn, Sakura and Takeo used their tantō to sever the camera wires, thus terminating the external camera feed. A large, bald man answered the door. He was younger and taller than Tatsuo, so he didn't detect any threat. Instead, he barked, "Who are you? Do you have an appointment?" Tatsuo did a slight, respectful bow, and as he straightened, he smashed his right fist into the man's lower jaw with a vicious uppercut. The man fell backwards, like a felled tree.

Immediately, Sakura stepped over him and fled up the first flight of steps. They were narrow, just wide enough for one person, typical in these older dwellings where space was at a premium. Her leather slippers were silent on the steps as she carefully placed each foot close to the walls on each tread to eliminate any boards squeaking. She moved swiftly, stopping when she reached the small platform where the next set of steps turned 180 degrees to climb up to the first level. She chose this landing to launch her attack. She would be hidden from anyone coming down the steps. Taking a deep breath, she calmed her mind and reached behind her shoulder, slowly drawing her tsurugi from its saya.

In her heightened state of awareness, she could hear a faint 'ting', the note the sword made when it was released from the saya. Then, a man yelled in Japanese, "Hey mother fucker, are you ok?" When there was no response, she could hear footsteps, moving quickly but not running. She also heard 'shush chunk', the sound of an automatic weapon chambering a round. This confirmed that the second guard was armed. Sakura waited silently, the tsurugi held tightly in both hands above her and to the right of her head, hardly breathing, as still as a statue.

First, she saw the barrel and then recognised the Beretta 92FS, a favoured weapon of the yakuza. When the hand and forearm holding the gun started to round the corner, she struck downwards in a smooth continuous diagonal stroke from above her right shoulder to her left thigh, stopping the motion when the sword was level with her left hip. This stroke is known as the Kesi Giri. She had practised this sword stroke daily during her ten years of training at the Sohei Temple. She had targeted the radio-carpal joint where the wrist joins the radius and the ulna, the two primary forearm bones. Only ligaments and cartilage hold this area together. The blade of her tsurugi severed the hand from the arm smoothly and without any loss of momentum.

The hand dropped to the ground, still holding the Beretta. The man screamed and continued around the platform, blood streaming from his arm stump. Sakura stepped quickly to face her opponent; he was a heavily tattooed yakuza mobster. His face was white from shock and his mouth opened wide as he screamed in pain. The screaming halted quickly as Sakura struck again, attacking the neck, the sword crossing from left to right, removing the head cleanly. A spray of arterial blood arced across the walls in the shape of a rainbow as the guard tumbled to the stairs, headless, sliding downwards towards the front door.

Sakura removed a plastic bag from a concealed pocket in her outfit, placed the head inside, pulled the ties closed and then attached it to a ring on the belt she wore around her waist. Next, she wiped the blade on her victim's shirt, removing most of the blood. Then, taking a silk cloth from her trousers, she wiped the blade clean before returning it to its saya.

She could see Takeo had secured cable ties to the wrists and ankles of the guard whom Tatsuo had knocked out earlier. He placed a hood over the man's head, then effortlessly hoisted the large guard onto his shoulder and walked outside to deposit him in the trunk of their car.

Sakura turned and climbed the steps to the first floor. Shoji doors accessed the four small rooms. She opened the first shoji door to see a man in his forties hastily put on his trousers. He turned when he heard the door slide open. Sakura scanned the room. There was a western-style bed and a naked girl lay on her back, her right wrist handcuffed to the headboard and her left ankle handcuffed to the footboard. Her eyes were opened but glassy, indicating she was heavily sedated. Sakura could feel her anger growing, a deep burning sensation in her stomach.

The man tried to push past her but she struck him hard with a roundhouse kick to the head, striking him in the temple. He dropped to the floor, unconscious. The skull's temple, or 'Pterion Bone', is located above the ear and is the joining point for four skull plates; this area is thin and fragile. Behind the Pterion bone is a major cranial artery called the middle meningeal artery. If this artery is severed, the skull cavity fills with blood causing severe pain; death can occur within hours. Sakura knew her kick was fatal. She had felt the skull shatter through her thin leather slippers. He would die without immediate medical attention. Yet, she felt no remorse. He deserved it.

She turned, left the room, and opened the door of the second room. An older man and a woman in her twenties were lying under a sheet, anxiously looking at Sakura as she entered the room.

Sakura spoke quietly in Japanese. "Are you here by force or by choice?"

The woman bowed her head and said, "Choice."

Sakura walked to the bed and yelled at the man, "Get up now!"

He quickly got out of bed. He was naked, hairy and fat. He stood trembling, covering his genitals with both hands. Sakura struck him with a punch to the jaw, and he spun around and fell to the floor, face down, unconscious. She drew her tsurugi sword, then drove it into the back of the man's neck, the blade slicing between the C3 and C4 vertebrae, severing his spinal cord. He would die in three minutes because his body no longer communicated with his brain. His breathing had already stopped.

"Now, give me the names of the people who run this operation."

The girl said, "They will kill me."

Sakura said, "If you don't tell me, I will kill you! They will never know. He won't tell them." Sakura pointed at the man lying on the floor to emphasise the point. The girl talked for several minutes providing information that Sakura recorded on her phone. Sakura had planned to kill the prostitute; however, after listening to her story, she felt empathetic towards her and decided to let her live. She was wearing her hood and mask so the woman would not be able to identify her but would only know she was a woman.

Sakura said, "Listen to me very carefully. The men who own this baishun yado will want to know who did this. I want you to tell them you were in the room with a client when you heard men yelling, 'Where do you keep the money?' Tell them your client got nervous. He tried to flee when two men entered the room. They killed him and raped you. Then they took the girl from the room next door. Can you be convincing?"

"Yes, of course I can; I must lie daily."

Sakura walked into the third room. It was separated into two areas: a dining area and the security office. The dining area had a small table, two chairs, and a bar fridge. The security side held three monitors; two were blacked out, probably the cameras they had disabled earlier. The third monitor showed the corridor, and she could see the bloodstained wall at the end of the hall. There didn't appear to be any other cameras and the security system was basic; no live feeds were going off-premises. Sakura accessed the control panel, searched backwards through the video to when she entered the corridor and deleted all the footage that contained images of her. Then she powered down the remaining camera.

There was an iPhone on the table. She picked it up; it could prove helpful. However, it was locked and required facial recognition. She removed the head from its bag and pointed it toward the iPhone. It took a few attempts before the phone opened. Entering the phone's settings, she reset the phone to open with a 6-digit PIN 111111. There was a locked drawer under the table supporting the security monitors. Sakura returned to the corridor and searched the dead guard's pockets until she found the key. The drawer contained JPY 2 million, the day's takings. She pocketed the money. She wanted this to look like a robbery gone wrong.

She walked into the fourth room, the bathroom, which contained a small shower and toilet and was surprisingly clean, with fresh towels for the clients to use when they had finished. No one was hiding in there. It was empty. Returning to the first room, she spoke softly to the young, sedated girl. "Can you hear me?" There was no reaction. She opened her lock-pick kit and selected a tool suitable to remove the handcuffs. Fifteen seconds later, the girl was free, the handcuffs no match for Sakura's lock-picking skills. As Takeo walked into the room, Sakura wrapped the bed sheet around the young girl to provide her with some warmth and privacy. He gently lifted the girl onto his shoulder and took her to their car.

ABOUT THE AUTHOR

I had *write a book* on my bucket list for several years. Retirement provided me with the time and opportunity. I have enjoyed reading since the age of twelve. Whilst my reading material has changed over the years, the stories I enjoy are those that keep me wanting to turn the next page.

I attempted to write a book where the reader would despise the villains yet consider the heroine's actions justified despite her methods including torture and violent death. I hope you think I achieved that.

I aimed to include only sufficient detail to describe the characters and locations but not to the extent that you would be thinking, "Come on, get on with it!" Achieving the balance of a rich story timeline without confusing the reader proved more difficult than I realised. The order of events and character introductions went though many iterations.

Sexual assault is a dreadful crime. I have tried to minimise the references to the assault and only include detail that supported the storyline. I wanted each of the murdered men to die in a way that reflected the sadistic nature of their crimes on Sakura and her mother.

In the beginning I felt my effort was amateurish and there were months where I wouldn't write at all. At night I would think about the book and characters and ideas would begin to flow reinvigorating me to continue. It took me a year to complete and whilst I know my writing skills are still amateurish I have enjoyed the process. I hope you enjoyed reading my first story of Sakura Bianchi.

I have since finished writing the second book in the series. In this story Sakura works to shut down a human trafficking operation in Japan.

ACKNOWLEDGEMENTS

I would like to thank my wife Michelle who read my early drafts and encouraged me to continue. She provided feedback on the characters and ideas that enriched the story.

As the book evolved I gained confidence and distributed it to close friends to 'test the water' so to speak. This was a period of anxiety for me but a necessary step to determine if the story was interesting.

I would like to thank Craig and Lorraine for reading the earlier drafts and providing me with encouragement to continue. Also my sister Vicky, Anastasia and Brian who read the near final drafts and provided feedback which improved the integrity of the story and characters. A big thank you to Marjorie Teoh who proofread and provided the final edits in the first release of the book.

In November 2023 I undertook an extensive revision. I am very grateful to Regina Smith who provided her time and experience to review and edit this final revision. Hopefully you won't find any errors, however if you do please contact me on author.paul.mcdonald@gmail.com.

Regards Paul